"Common Sense Tells Me To Walk Away Now," Emma Whispered. "You Have A Reputation For Never Going Out With An Employee."

"I never have," Zach answered. "That doesn't mean I can't."

"That wasn't what I wanted to hear. I ̶̶̶̶̶̶̶̶̶̶"

"Don't quit on me," he ̶̶̶̶̶̶̶̶̶̶ quiet. A muscle wo ̶̶̶̶̶̶̶̶̶̶ salary."

"Double my salary?" ̶̶̶̶̶̶̶̶̶̶ head.

"You don't need to pa ̶̶̶̶̶̶̶̶̶̶ on't walk out over a few casual kisses."

Exasperated and stung over his dismissal of kisses that had shaken her, she stared at him. "Those kisses weren't casual to my way of thinking," she whispered.

She stepped close, put her arm around his neck and placed her mouth on his, kissing him with all the heat and fury she felt over his dismissive attitude. In seconds, she broke off the kiss and looked up with satisfaction.

"I'd say your body's reaction isn't *casual,* either," she said, catching her breath.

Dear Reader,

Depending on circumstances, holidays can be painful or joyous, and *Midnight Under the Mistletoe* is about those opposing feelings.

For some, Christmas is a family celebration. It is a kaleidoscope of events and people, funny moments, happy ones, touching occasions, unpredictable occurrences and as the years go by, the holiday is laced with memories of loved ones and good times. This story, as well as one of the characters, reflects that view of Christmas. Also, the story is about the breaking away of the hardened shell of someone's hurt and loneliness acquired through too many disappointing childhood Christmases.

Watch handsome billionaire Texan Zach Delaney's life transform when Emma Hillman pours her love of Christmas into his life. His stunning secretary, who is a total opposite in personality and completely off-limits to him, becomes the biggest temptation of his life. What happens when a man who has always skipped Christmas falls in love with a woman who is the embodiment of the December celebration?

Thank you for selecting *Midnight Under the Mistletoe*. Happy holidays to all!

Sara Orwig

SARA ORWIG

MIDNIGHT UNDER THE MISTLETOE

HARLEQUIN®

entertain, enrich, inspire™

Recycling programs
for this product may
not exist in your area.

ISBN-13: 978-0-373-73208-1

MIDNIGHT UNDER THE MISTLETOE

www.Harlequin.com

Printed in U.S.A.

SARA ORWIG

lives in Oklahoma. She has a patient husband who will take her on research trips anywhere from big cities to old forts. She is an avid collector of Western history books. With a master's degree in English, Sara has written historical romance, mainstream fiction and contemporary romance. Books are beloved treasures that take Sara to magical worlds, and she loves both reading and writing them.

With special thanks to
Stacy Boyd, Shana Smith and Maureen Walters.
May you have a blessed and joyous holiday.

One

Another secretary to interview.

Zach Delaney stood at the window of his west Texas ranch and watched the approaching car. This candidate was prompt. He had heard this one lived in Dallas, was single, only twenty-four, a homebody who insisted on weekends free to go home. She wanted a week off before Christmas and two days after Christmas. If she could do the work, it was all right with him. He didn't know her, but she had worked more than two years at his Dallas office, which held the corporate offices of his demolition company, his trucking company and the architectural firm he owned. She'd risen fast and was highly recommended.

As Zach watched the car approach the house, he thought about the other secretaries he'd interviewed and the conversation he'd had with his brother Will, who had stopped by an hour ago.

He remembered Will laughing. "I know you—you're probably about to go up in smoke from boredom."

"You've got that right. I feel as if I'm a prisoner and time seems to have stopped," Zach replied, raking his fingers through his thick, brown curls.

Will nodded. "Don't forget—you're supposed to stay off your feet and keep your foot elevated."

"I'm doing that most of the time. Believe me, I want my foot to get well."

Will smiled. "You should have just stayed in Dallas after Garrett's wedding earlier this month. You haven't been cooped up like this since you were five and had the mumps."

"Don't remind me."

"That was twenty-seven years ago. I don't know how you've made it this long in demolition without getting hurt."

"I've been lucky and careful, I guess."

"If you don't end up hiring today's interviewee, I'll send someone out to work for you. If I had known the difficulty you're having finding a competent secretary, I would have sent one before now."

"Thanks. One secretary lasted a few days before deciding the ranch was too isolated. Another talked incessantly," Zach grumbled, causing Will to laugh. His brother's brown eyes sparkled with amusement.

"One of those women hovered over me and told me what to do to take care of myself. Actually, Will, instead of hiring a secretary to help go through Dad's stuff, maybe we should just trash it all. Dad's been gone almost a year now and this stuff hasn't been touched. It's not important. The only value that stuff can have is sentimental. That makes it worthless as time passes."

"We don't know for sure there isn't something of value in those boxes," Will argued.

Zach nodded. "Knowing our father, he could have put some vital papers, money or something priceless in these boxes, just so someone *would* have to wade through them."

"You volunteered to go through his papers while you recuperate from your fall. You don't have to."

"I'll do it. The secretary will help go through all the letters and memorabilia while I also keep up with work. You became guardian for Caroline and you handled a lot of the dealings to bring our half sister into the family. Ryan's knee-deep in getting his new barn built while commuting back and forth to his business in Houston. Besides, I'm the one incapacitated with time on my hands. I'm it, for now. I don't know what got into Dad, keeping all this memorabilia. He would never have actually written a family history."

"Our father was not one you could figure. His actions were unfathomable except for making money. He probably intended to write a family history. In his old age I think he became nostalgic." Will headed toward the door and then paused. "You sure you don't want to join us for Thanksgiving? I'll send someone to get you," he added, and Zach was touched by Will's concern.

"Thanks, but no thanks. You enjoy Ava's family. Ryan leaves soon to spend Thanksgiving with the latest woman in his life—I can't keep up with which one this is. I'll be fine and enjoy myself all by myself."

"If you change your mind, let me know. Also, it's less than six weeks until Christmas. We're going to Colorado for the holiday. Do you want to come along? We'll be happy to have you join us."

"Thank you." Zach grinned. "I think I'll go to the house in Italy. It'll be beautiful there and you know I don't do Christmas."

"So who is the beautiful Italian lady? I'm sure there is one."

"Might be more than one." Zach smiled. "You hadn't been into Christmas much yourself until you got Caroline. Now you have to celebrate."

"Truthfully, with Caroline, it's been fun. Come with us and you'll see."

"I love little Caroline, but you go ahead. Doc told me to stay put and this is a better place than snowy mountains in Colorado."

"That's true, but we'd take care of you."

Zach shook his head. "Thanks, Will, for coming out."

"Let me know about the secretary. I'll get you one who's excellent."

"With Margo on maternity leave, I may have to find a new one permanently. I don't want to think about that."

Now, Zach shifted his foot and glared at it, recalling the moment the pile of rubble had given way and he had fallen, breaking an ankle, plus small bones, causing a sprain and getting one deep gash. Staying off his foot most of the time was hell. He didn't like working daily in an office, and the doctor told him he couldn't go back to working on site or travel much, but he could do some work at the ranch and stay off his foot as best he could.

Zach sighed as the car slowed in front of the house. Emma Hillman. She climbed out of her car and came up the walk.

Startled, he momentarily forgot her mission. A tall, wind-blown, leggy redhead, who would turn heads everywhere, was striding toward his front door. With looks like hers, she belonged on a model's catwalk or doing a commercial or in a bar, not striding purposefully toward his house in the hopes of doing secretarial chores. Even though she wore a tailored, dark green suit with an open black coat over it, she had a wild, attention-getting appearance.

The west Texas wind swept over her, catching more tendrils of long red hair and blowing them around her face. Immobilized, Zach stared. She didn't look like any secretary on his staff in any office he had. Nor did she resemble the homebody type to his way of thinking. All those recommendations she had—they must have been based on her looks. His spirits sank. He would have to ask Will to find him somebody else. He needed someone who would stay on the ranch during the week. This one was a declared homebody. Add that to her looks and he couldn't imagine it working out. He also couldn't imagine her being an efficient secretary, either. He would give Emma Hillman a lot of work and in less than two days, she would probably fold and run as her predecessor had.

When the bell rang, he could hear Nigel get the door. Zach hobbled back to the middle of the room to wait to meet her. Before he sent her packing, he might get her home phone number. Actually, even if she did work out here, when the temporary job ended she'd go back to the corporate office, so getting her phone number was only wishful thinking. She'd still be an employee. Even so, eagerness to meet her took the boredom out of the morning. This promised to be his most enjoyable moment since he arrived at the ranch.

Emma Hillman pushed a button and heard chimes. Her gaze swept over the large porch. The ranch was not at all what she had pictured in her mind. She had expected a rustic, sprawling house, not a mansion that bordered on palatial. When the door swung open, she faced a slender gray-haired man.

"Welcome, Miss Hillman?"

"Yes," she said, entering as he stepped back.

"I'm Nigel Smith. If you'll come with me, Mr. Delaney is waiting."

Following him, she glanced around the enormous entrance. Wood floors had a dark appearance with a treatment that gave them an antiqued quality and probably would not show boot marks or much of anything else.

She tried to finger-comb her hair and tuck tendrils back into the clips that held her hair on either side of her head. She had been warned about Zach Delaney—that he was difficult to please, curt, all business. Actually, he had conflicting descriptions—a charismatic hunk by some; others pronounced him a demanding ogre. She had been told too many times about her three predecessors who hadn't lasted more than a day or two.

She didn't care—it was a fabulous opportunity for another promotion in the company and the pay was terrific right at Christmastime. Even though she was going to miss being in Dallas with her family, she was determined to cooperate with Zach Delaney and be the secretary who got to stay.

Nigel led her through an open door into a large room with shelves of books on two walls, a huge fireplace on another and all glass on the fourth. In a hasty glance she barely saw any of her surroundings because her attention was ensnared by the tall man standing in the center of the room.

His prominent cheekbones and a firm jaw were transformed by a mass of dark brown curls and riveting blue eyes. A black knit shirt and tight jeans revealed muscles and a fit physique. Even standing quietly, he appeared commanding.

Dimly, she heard Nigel present her and she thanked him as he left, but her gaze was locked with the head of her company, Zach Delaney. Her breathing altered, her heart raced and her palms became damp. She felt flustered, drawn to him, unable to look away. For heartbeats, they gazed at each other while silence stretched.

With an effort she offered her hand. "I'm glad to meet you, Mr. Delaney," she said. Her voice was soft in her ears.

He stepped forward, his hand closing around hers, his warm fingers breaking the spell she had been temporarily enveloped in. "Welcome to the Delaney ranch. I'm happy to meet you, and it's Zach. We're going to work closely together. No 'Mr. Delaney.' And please have a seat." His voice was deep, warm and sexy, an entertainer's voice.

Feeling foolish, yet unable to control the physical reaction she was having to him, she sat in a leather chair. Another chair was close and he turned it to face her, sitting near her. "I've read your recommendations, which are excellent. If you want this job, you're to move here for the duration of the time you work for me—five, possibly six weeks total. Your weekends are free from one on Friday afternoon until Monday morning at nine o'clock."

"That's fine with me," she replied, thinking someone should have warned her about his appeal. He rarely was in the Dallas office and executive offices were on the top floor. She had never seen him or crossed paths with him before. She had no idea she would have such an intense reaction to meeting him.

"I expect this job to end around Christmas, when my foot heals. You can return to the Dallas office and I will be on my way back to the field."

"Fine," she replied, barely able to concentrate on what he was saying for getting lost in vivid blue eyes. His conversation might have been practical, all business, but the look in his eyes was not. Blue depths probed, examined and conveyed a sensual appraisal that shimmied warmly over her nerves. "As I mentioned in our phone call, I'd like to take that week before Christmas and two days afterward if the job hasn't ended."

"That's fine. As far as your duties, you're here to help with any correspondence or business matters I have and to help me sort through some family papers. My father intended to write a family history. He had old letters and family memorabilia that have been passed through generations, that sort of thing. I volunteered to go through all of it while I'm supposed to stay off my feet," Zach said, waving his hand toward the boxes of papers nearby.

"The memorabilia should be fascinating," she remarked.

"If your ancestors wrote these letters and sent them, how did they get possession of them again?"

"Good question. They wrote other relatives, sisters, brothers, and as far as I can see, everybody saved every word that was put on paper. There are letters in those boxes that aren't from Delaneys, but are written to a Delaney who saved it. You'd think one person would have tossed them. If the letter isn't from a Delaney, there is no reason to keep it."

"I imagine some were tossed. There were probably more since you had such prolific writers in your family."

"If I were the only Delaney of my generation, I would simply shred the papers this week because I think they're junk. Some of the letters date back to the 1800s."

Horrified at the thought of shredding old letters, she stared at him. "The 1800s? It should be spellbinding to read about your relatives," she blurted before she thought about how it might sound critical of her boss's attitude.

He smiled. "I suppose it's a good thing you feel that way because you'll be reading some of this stuff for me. Anyway, that in general is what I hired you to do. Does this sound acceptable?"

"Certainly. I'm looking forward to it."

"Great. Feel free to ask questions at any time. I'll have Nigel see about getting you moved in. You were asked to come prepared to move in. Is this what you did?"

"Yes. I was told to pack for the job because you might hire me and want me to stay."

"I'm getting desperate for a secretary. The salary should make up for some of the demands," he said and she merely nodded.

"Nigel is sort of jack-of-all-trades around the house. He acts as butler, assistant and a financial manager. You'll meet more of our staff, who have homes on the ranch."

"I wonder if I'll ever find my way around," she said as she glanced beyond him toward the hall.

"Nigel will give you a map of the house. We have an indoor pool and one outside. Feel free to swim after or before work hours. We have a gym, too."

"This is a modernized ranch home."

"This house has been remodeled many times. The family room was the actual original house, built in the 1800s. Anyway, my grandfather had an elevator installed, so I'm taking it temporarily. You're welcome to if you want."

"Thank you, I won't need the elevator," she replied with a smile. "I exercise each day, so stairs are good."

"Great. Do you think we can start work this morning in about an hour?"

"Certainly."

As he stood, she came to her feet and followed him to the door. He offered his hand. "Welcome to the Delaney ranch, Emma," he drawled in a mesmerizing voice that wrapped around her like a warm blanket. She shook hands again with him, an electric current flashing from the contact while she looked into the bluest eyes she had ever seen. Dark brown curly lashes framed his mesmerizing eyes.

"I hope you find your stay here worthwhile," he said, a dry, professional statement, but his tone of voice, with those blue eyes focused on her and her hand enveloped in his, made her think of sizzling kisses. Realizing how she was staring, she withdrew her hand and stepped back. He turned to walk into the hall to talk to Nigel, nodded at her, and in seconds she left with Nigel to see where she would stay.

The next hour was a whirlwind of getting unpacked enough to function through the day. To her surprise she had more than a room—it was a suite with a sitting area, a dream bedroom with a four-poster and fruitwood furniture. Dazzled by the lavish quarters, she looked at a bathroom as large as her apartment. The bath held a sunken tub, potted plants, mirrors, an adjoining dressing room plus a huge walk-in closet. She took pictures on her cell phone to send to her sisters. She could imagine how they would ooh and aah over where she was staying. Her paramount concern was how would she work constantly around Zach Delaney. She had heard rumors at the office about how appealing he was, but not from anyone who had actually worked for him. She had talked to one secretary who had spent two days with him and thought he was a monster, piling on work until it was impossible to get done what he demanded. Another secretary had complained about him being silent and abrupt during the day.

When she saw it was time to go back to meet with him, she smoothed her hair into a loose bun and left her room. Trying to familiarize herself with the mansion, she walked to the study where she had met Zach.

He sat behind a desk and stood the minute she appeared in the doorway. Once again, she tried to avoid staring. He looked muscled and fit except for his foot that was wrapped in a bandage and in an oversize health shoe. The unruly curls were a tangle around his face, softening his rugged features.

"Let's go to the office," he said, and she walked beside him down a wide hall filled with paintings, plants, side tables and chairs.

As they entered a large room, she drew a deep breath. It was a dream office with two large desks at opposite ends of the room. Shelves lined three walls and the remaining wall was glass with a view of a small pond and well tended grounds up to a white fence. Beyond the fence were stables, a corral and pasture. Through spacious windows, daylight spilled into the room. Fax machines, shredders, computers and electronic equipment filled each end of the office.

"That's my desk," he said, pointing to the larger one that was polished, ornately carved dark wood. Forming an Lshape with the desk, a table stood at one end. The table held two computers, one of which had dual oversize monitors. Another computer was centered on his desk. Two laptops and an iPad lay on the table.

The other desk was glass, looking far newer. File cabinets were built into one wall and not noticeable at first glance.

He sat behind his desk, motioning toward a leather chair facing him. She sat, crossing her legs, catching him looking at her legs when she glanced up. She inhaled sharply. She experienced an undercurrent of intense awareness and suspected he did as well. It was unexpected, definitely unwanted. Any hot attraction between them could put her job in jeopardy and this job was important to her. She was saving to go back to college and, ultimately, become qualified to teach. This was a temporary increase in pay she could use to achieve her dream.

"Since you and I and my staff are the only people here, you can dress casually. Jeans are fine."

She nodded. "Great."

"The glass desk will be yours. You'll find a stack of papers I've signed that need to be copied and put into the mail." He leaned back and stretched out his long legs.

She realized she was going to have a difficult time for a few days, focusing on what he was saying because she got lost looking at him.

"Hopefully you'll be able to read my handwriting. I have a document there for you to type for me to sign. Another stack holds filing. There's an in-box on the corner of my desk. When you finish anything, if it doesn't go in the mail or the file, place it in my in-box. If you have any questions, always feel free to ask. Take a break when you want and feel free to get what you want in the kitchen. Did Nigel show you where the kitchen is?"

"Yes, he showed me around briefly."

"Did you meet my very good cook?"

"Yes, I met Rosie."

"Good. You can start work each day at 8:00, quit at 4:00 or start at 9:00 and quit at 5:00. You're stuck here for lunch so we'll not add that to the time."

"I prefer 8:00," she said and he nodded.

"Any questions now?" he asked, giving her a direct look that made her pulse jump another notch.

"One—where do I take the mail?"

"There's a box on a shelf near your desk that is marked Mail and you put everything in there. One of the hands who works on the ranch will get the mail to take it down to the road to be picked up."

She nodded and headed over to her desk, feeling her back prickle because she suspected Zach's gaze was on her. She sat down and looked at the piles of work in front of her, remembering the angry statements from Brenna about Zach Delaney heaping mountains of work on her. It looked like a lot now—hopefully, by the end of the day, she would have made a big enough dent in the stacks to get to keep this job.

Still conscious of him across the room, Emma reached for a stack. As she began to read the first letter, she tried to keep from glancing his way. She pushed the stack aside and picked up a tablet with a bold handwriting. The writing to be typed looked the most time-consuming, so she started with it. In minutes she managed to put Zach out of her thoughts.

When she finished each task, she placed it in the proper pile. Standing, she gathered the work she had completed and put papers for Zach into his in-box. His back was turned as he worked at his computer and she looked at the thick hair curling on the back of his head.

She had not expected to be working in the same room with him. Also, she hadn't expected to work for someone who took her breath and set her pulse racing just by a glance from his sky-blue eyes.

With a deep sigh, she placed letters in the box for mail and then she started to file.

She looked across the room to see him setting papers in a pile. He picked up the letters in his in-box, glanced at her to catch her watching him again. She turned away to work on her computer, in seconds concentrating on what she was doing for the next half hour. She finished another stack and picked them up to take to his in-box and this time when she glanced his way, she met his gaze.

He seemed to be sitting and watching her. She picked up the papers and carried them to his desk, all the time aware of his steady observation.

As she started to put the letters into the box, he took them and riffled through them before looking at her. "You're a fast worker. And an accurate one."

"Thank you. I try to be."

"I figured with all the work I've piled on you this morning, you'd be out of here as fast as the others."

"I intend to stay," she said, amused, and realizing he might have been testing to see how she worked. She went back to her desk, again having that tingly feeling across her shoulders, certain he was watching her.

When she glanced at him, he had settled back to read. In seconds, he placed the letter in the stack beside him on his desk.

What kind of man did she work for? When she had gone to work at Z.A.D. Enterprises, she hadn't given much thought to the head of the business because she'd heard he was rarely in the Dallas office. The business comprised primarily of demolition, but also had a trucking company, an architectural firm and a concrete company. The international company had offices scattered worldwide and she heard Zachary Delaney traveled constantly from site to site, something she would detest. Other than that and the recent grumbling by Brenna, she knew little about him. Not one of the secretaries who had preceded her had said anything about his appeal, about his looks, about anything except he had proven difficult to work for. Maya, as well as Brenna, had thought he was unreceptive and uncommunicative. All had complained the workload was too heavy and she had to agree it was a lot, but it made time fly. On the other hand, around the office the word had always been that he was friendly. Perhaps part of his surly reputation with some secretaries was caused by his being injured and isolated on a ranch.

She returned to the stack, until she heard the scrape of a chair.

He stood and stretched, flexing muscles in his arms. When he glanced her way, she was embarrassed to be caught staring at him again.

"Want some lunch?" Without waiting for her answer, he motioned. "C'mon, we'll get something to eat. Rosie will have something fixed."

"Thank you," she said. "I still have letters, though."

"C'mon. You'll like Rosie's cooking and she'll be disappointed if you don't come eat. Those letters aren't urgent."

"Very well. You're the boss and I don't want to hurt her feelings." Glancing at her watch, Emma was surprised it was half past twelve. "I didn't realize the time."

"Time flies when you're having fun," he said, grinning at her. Creases appeared on either side of his mouth in an enticing smile that caused her to smile in return.

"So, Emma, tell me about yourself since we'll be working together for the next month or so."

Satisfaction flared because he must mean she would get to stay. "There's not much to tell. I've been at Z.A.D. for two years now. I have an apartment in Dallas and have two sisters and two brothers. My sisters, Sierra and Mary Kate, and Connor, my older brother, are married. Bobby and I are single. What about you?"

"I have two brothers, it was three, one is deceased. My older brother became guardian of our little niece, Caroline."

"That's sad. Is your niece's mother deceased, too?"

"No, her mother walked out when Caroline was a baby. She didn't want to be tied down with responsibilities, although she had a nanny and someone to cook and clean."

"I can't imagine," Emma said, staring at him.

He shrugged. "One more thing to sour me on marriage. My older brother felt the same way until this year. He just married in September."

"You don't want to get married and have a family?"

His mouth quirked in a crooked smile. "Not even remotely. The weeks I'm spending here recuperating are probably the longest I've stayed home in Texas in I don't know when. I'm a traveler."

"I've heard you work all over the world and I know Z.A.D. has offices worldwide. I have a vastly different life. I don't want to miss a weekend with my family."

"We're poles apart there," he remarked with a smile, directing her into a large kitchen with an adjoining dining room that held a table and chairs, a sofa, a fireplace, two wingback chairs and a bar.

"What's for lunch, Rosie? Something smells tempting," he said, raising a lid on a pot on the stove. A stocky woman in a uniform bustled around the kitchen. Her graying hair was in a bun and glasses perched on her turned-up nose.

"Chicken soup there and I have quesadillas or turkey melt sandwiches—your preference."

"How about soup, plus—" He paused and looked questioningly at Emma. "Either of the choices have any appeal?"

"Of course. Quesadillas, please."

"Good choice. Rosie's are special. Soup and quesadillas it is. We can help ourselves, Rosie."

Bowls and plates were on the counter. With that steady awareness of him at her side, Emma helped herself to a small bowl of soup, surprised when Zach set down his dishes and held her chair as she sat down. The gesture made their lunch together seem far less like boss and secretary eating together than a man and a woman on a date. Rosie appeared with a coffeepot, which Emma declined and Zach accepted.

When he sat, she said, "I'm sure everyone asks, what drew you to demolition?"

"A child's love of tearing something down, probably. I have an engineering degree and I almost went to architecture school. I have architects working for me so we build where we tear down. We build sometimes where nothing has stood. I find it fascinating work."

"I hear you go all over the world." She didn't add that she knew he was wealthy enough he would never have to work a day if he didn't want to.

The Delaney wealth was well publicized. She had never known anyone like him before. His love of travel was foreign to her. His disregard for family and marriage dismayed her even more than his apparent disregard for his family history. He had a lifestyle she could not imagine, but the head of the company was light-years from her clerical job, which provided an excellent way to save money to finish her college education.

"So, Zach, your favorite locale is where?" she asked as Rosie brought a platter with steaming quesadillas to set between them.

"There's too many to have a favorite. I love Paris, I love Torres del Paine, Iguazu Falls, the city of New York. They're all interesting. Where's your favorite?"

"Home with my family," she said, smiling at him, and he shook his head.

"Okay, I'll rephrase my question," he said. "Where's your favorite place outside of Texas?"

She lowered her fork. "I've never been outside of Texas."

One dark eyebrow arched as surprise flashed briefly in his blue eyes. "Never been outside of Texas," he repeated, studying her as if she had announced she had another set of ears beneath her red hair.

"No, I'm happy here."

"You might be missing something," he said, still scrutinizing her with open curiosity.

"I don't think so, therefore, that's really all that matters, right?" she asked, certain after today he would have satisfied his curiosity about her and lunch with the boss would cease.

"You're missing some wonderful places and you don't even know it."

She smiled at him again, thinking he might be missing some wonderful family companionship and didn't even know it. "As long as I'm content, it doesn't matter."

"So tell me about this family of yours and what they all do."

"My family lives near me in Dallas. Dad is an accountant and my mom is a secretary. My younger brother works part-time and is in school at the University of North Texas. I've taken classes to become a teacher. This semester I didn't enroll, but I hope to start back soon."

"How far along are you?"

"I have a little more than half the credits I need. Back to my family—in addition to my siblings, I have five small nieces and three nephews. We have assorted other relatives, grandparents, aunts and uncles, who live in the same general area."

"Big family."

"My siblings and I visit my parents on weekends," she said.

"So do my aunts and uncles. There are anywhere from twenty to thirty or forty of us when we all get together."

He paused as he started to drink his water, giving her a polite smile as if she said they spent every weekend at the park so they could play on the slides and swings.

"My family is definitely not that together," he said. "We go our separate ways. Dad's deceased and Mom disappeared from our lives when we were young."

"We have different lifestyles," she said, thinking this was a man she couldn't possibly ever be close to even if circumstances had been different. His world and hers were poles apart. Their families were so different—hers a huge part of her life, his nearly nonexistent, what with his father being deceased and his mother walking out years earlier. Those events had to influence him and make him the man he was today. This job would be brief and then she probably would never see him again. "The quesadilla is delicious," she said.

"I told you Rosie is a good cook. So, is there any special person in your life right now? I assume no one objected to you taking this job."

"Not at all and there's no special person at the moment. As long as I can go home for the weekends and holidays, I'm fine."

"I'm not sure I've been involved—friends or otherwise—with someone as tied into home and family."

"I'm your secretary—that's different from your women friends."

"We can be friends," he said, looking amused, and a tingle ran across her nerves. In tiny subtle ways he was changing their relationship from professional to personal, something she did not want. With every discovery about him, she saw what opposites they were. This was not a man who would ever fit into her world or her life other than on a physical level. She definitely did not fit into his.

Surprised that he was even interested, she had to wonder. She had never heard a word of gossip about him even remotely trying to have an outside relationship with an employee. Far from it—occasional remarks were made to new single women to forget about impressing the boss—if they even got to know him—except through efficient work.

"We can be friends to a degree in a professional manner," she said, wondering if she sounded prim.

"Emma, we're going to be under the same roof, working together for weeks. Relax. This isn't the office and it's not that formal. If I have something critical, a letter I just have to get out, an appointment that has to be made by a certain time, I'll tell you."

"Fair enough," she said, feeling as if their relationship just made another subtle shift. Or was it her imagination because she found him so physically attractive? "So you don't gather often with the family, you travel a lot—what else do you do?"

"Most of the time for the past few years my life has been tied up in my work. I have a yacht, but I'm seldom on it. I ski. I have a villa in Italy. I have a condo in New York, one in Chicago and I spend the most time between Paris and Chicago where we have offices. I like cities."

She placed her fork across her plate and stood. "That was a delicious lunch. If you'll excuse me, I should get back to the letters."

"Sit and relax, Emma. Those letters aren't urgent and they'll be there after lunch. I'm enjoying talking to you. There's no rush. And I suspect some tidbit will appear for dessert."

Surprised, she sat again. "I'm not in the habit of arguing with my supervisor. I don't think I can possibly eat dessert. This was more lunch than I usually have."

"Indulge yourself while you can," he said. Pushing his plate forward, he placed his arms on the table and leaned closer. "Emma, this is lunch. We're not at work. Forget the supervisor-secretary relationship, which doesn't have to exist 24/7. This is just two people having lunch together," he drawled in that husky voice that was soft as fur. Vivid blue eyes held her attention while his words poured over her and the moment shifted, holding a cozy intimacy. "Beautiful green eyes, great red hair—they sort of lend themselves to forgetting all about business," he said softly.

"We're about to cross a line we shouldn't cross," she whispered while her heart hammered.

"We crossed that line when you came in the door," he replied.

Two

Her heart thudded because his words changed their relationship. She realized her reply would set the standard. For a fleeting second, how tempted she was to flirt back, to give him a seductive reply that was on the tip of her tongue. For the moment, she wished he were someone else and not her boss.

Following the path of wisdom, practicality and caution, she smiled and chuckled, shaking her head and trying to diffuse the electrifying tension that had sprung between them. "I don't think so," she replied lightly. "We can't. I'm here for a secretarial job, which sets definite limits. I'm not crossing that line. If that's part of my work—then tell me now."

"Definitely not part of the job," he said, leaning back and studying her with a faint smile and amusement dancing in his blue eyes. "As rare for me as for you in an employer-employee situation. But we're not going to be able to shut it off that easily. As a matter of fact, I think the chemistry is in spite of both of us, not because of either of us wanting it to happen. That's a big difference and rather fascinating."

"We'll not pursue it," she persisted. Rosie appeared with a tray that held four choices of desserts. "What would you like, Miss Hillman?" she asked.

"Please just call me Emma," she said, looking at luscious desserts. She was no longer hungry, yet Rosie stood with a broad smile and Emma knew how her own mother liked for everyone to take some of her desserts, so she selected a small slice of chocolate cheesecake.

Zach took a monstrous concoction of vanilla ice cream and brownies topped with fudge sauce with a sprinkling of fresh raspberries.

"You must work out big-time to turn that into muscle," she observed and the moment the words were spoken, she wished she could take them back because she had just tossed the conversation back to the personal. "This is so much food. What does Rosie do with leftovers? Save them for dinner?" Emma interjected, trying to get the conversation on a different note as rapidly as possible.

He flashed a slight smile as he shook his head. "I work out and my injured foot has thrown me off schedule. As for the leftovers—there are a lot of people on this ranch. She'll pass them on after lunch and they'll be gone by midafternoon. You think all those hungry cowboys won't light into her cooking? They'll devour it."

She smiled, glad the moment had been diffused and they were back on a harmless topic. "This is delicious," she said as she ate a bite. She looked up to meet his steady gaze that fluttered her insides.

"She'll be glad to know you liked it. Rosie's been cooking for us since I was a little kid."

She smiled and they enjoyed their desserts, then she said, "Do you mind if I put a few family pictures on my desk?"

"Emma, within reason, put whatever you want on your desk or around your desk or in your room upstairs. I don't care what you do unless you want to paint something or make a permanent change."

"Of course not. Thanks. Now, if you'll excuse me, I think this time I will get back to work," she said, folding her napkin and standing. When she picked up her plate, he touched her wrist lightly.

"Leave the dishes or you'll get a Rosie lecture. She's in charge here and she wants to do things herself and her way," he said, releasing her wrist as he stood and walked around the table.

Smiling, she set her plate down. "I know how my mother and one of my sisters are. Sometimes they just want all of us out of the kitchen."

"You're so tied into your family. Are you going to be able to stay away from Dallas for the length of this job?"

"I gave that some serious thought, but this isn't permanent and as far as I can see, this assignment is a great opportunity because it's a hike in pay, even temporarily, and I'm saving money to finish my education. And I did ask for the weekends off to go home."

"We both hope it works out. So far, so good. I'll admit, I didn't expect you to last the morning, because several before you didn't. I've been pleasantly surprised."

"Glad to hear I'm up to snuff. So far so good in working for you," she replied with a smile.

One dark eyebrow arched quizzically as he looked down at her. "You expected an ogre. Aah—let me guess—rumors from your predecessors."

Still smiling, she nodded. They entered the office and she left to return to the correspondence and filing. Within the hour she noticed he had stopped heaping work for her and she could see where she would catch up with all he had given her.

No matter how lost she got in the assignments, she couldn't shake her awareness of him. Carrying papers to his desk, she often met his gaze while he talked on the phone. Each time it was the same as a physical contact with a sizzle.

Common sense warned this job would not be as simple and straightforward as she had envisioned. When he talked on the phone, his voice was usually low enough that she couldn't hear much of what he was saying and she made no effort to try to hear. She caught snatches of words, enough to know he was discussing problems involving his work.

As she placed a letter in the box for mail, Zach got off his phone. "Emma, take a break. The afternoon is more than half gone."

"I'm fine."

"Take a break—walk around the place, go outside, go to the kitchen and get a snack—whatever you want to do. Don't argue or I'll come get you and we'll go for a stroll. As much as I can stroll right now."

She laughed. "What a threat," she said, placing mail in the box and hurrying out of the room as she received a grin from him. She hoped he didn't guess moments like that played havoc with her insides. How tempting to head back to work just to get him to spend the next few minutes with her.

She stood in the wide, empty hall and wondered what to do, finally going toward the kitchen to get a cup of tea. She suspected there was a very well-stocked pantry.

"Afternoon, Emma," Rosie greeted her.

"It smells wonderful in here."

"Roast for dinner. Can I get you something?"

"Yes, thank you. If possible, I'd like a cup of hot tea."

"Of course," Rosie replied. "Looks as if you might be the one who stays."

"I hope so."

Rosie chuckled. "Those others looked frazzled and unhappy from the first morning. I would have sent one packing faster than Zach did. Have a seat and I'll brew your tea—or if you want a breath of fresh air, go outside and I'll bring it to you."

"Thanks, Rosie."

"You can take it back to your desk if you want. Zach isn't particular about food in the office if you don't leave crumbs or make a big mess."

"I won't," Emma replied, smiling. "I'll wait outside," she added, stepping out onto the patio and strolling to the pool to look at the crystal water that was almost the same blue as Zach's eyes.

When she finished her tea, she went to her room to retrieve a small box of family pictures. She had already distributed some pictures in the bedroom. When instructed to arrive with her things packed she had brought what she really wanted with her. She stopped to look around again, still amazed at the size and beauty of where she would stay.

When she returned to her desk, Zach was on the phone and she had more work waiting. After placing her pictures on her desk and table, she focused on correspondence, so lost in concentration she was startled when Zach spoke to her.

"It's half past five. Just because the work is here in the house, you don't need to stay all hours. We'll close the office now. I eat a late dinner, but you can eat whenever you want—Rosie will be in the kitchen until eight. After that she'll have cold or easily heated choices on a chalkboard menu."

"Thanks," she said, wondering if she had eaten her last meal with the boss. If she had, it would be the wisest thing to happen. At the same time, she couldn't prevent her slight disappointment.

"You've done good work today, Emma. I hope you like the job."

She wanted to laugh and say that he sounded surprised. Instead, she merely nodded. "Thank you. I think this will be good."

He gave her a long look that killed the impersonal moments that had just passed. Once again her nerves tingled, invisible sparks danced in the air and she could feel heat rising. In spite of logic, she didn't want him to go.

Turning away, he walked out of the room without saying anything further. She stared at the empty doorway. The chemistry had not changed. He seemed to fight it as much as she, which was a relief and made the situation easier.

Zach continued to pile on a lot of work. While there wasn't as much as that first morning, letters to write, papers to proof, appointments to set, phone calls and various tasks streamed to her desk. Time passed swiftly as she worked diligently and kept up with what he sent to her. There were no more lunches together. Sometimes he worked straight through and then stopped about four. Sometimes he ate at his desk. He continued to make an effort to keep their relationship impersonal, which suited her completely. No matter how cool he was, there still was no way to stop that acute consciousness she had of him as an appealing male.

Thursday the work he gave her in the morning was done by noon. When she returned after lunch he sat by a large cardboard box filled with papers.

"Want to tackle some of the old letters and memorabilia?"

"Sure," she replied, watching him pull another chair near his. "That's a lot of letters."

"Many were written by my great-great-grandfather to his sister, his brother, later his wife. They were all saved and somehow ended up back with our family. Probably some relative didn't want them and another one took them."

"Zach, that's wonderful. I'd think you'd want to read each of these yourself."

"Hardly. They are letters from an old codger who settled out here and struggled to carve out a life on the plains. He was probably a tough old bird and about as lovable as a prickly porcupine. I think you are romanticizing him. Sit here beside me so whenever you have a question you can ask me. Want anything to drink before we start?"

"No, thank you, I'm fine." As she crossed the room, his gaze raked briefly over her, making every inch tingle. She became aware of the navy sweater and matching slacks she had pulled on this morning, her hair in a ponytail.

Catching a whiff of his enticing aftershave, she sat beside him.

"The big basket is for letters and papers that go to the shredder," he instructed. Sitting only inches from him, she was lost in his blue eyes and could barely focus on what he told her. She was even closer than she had been that first morning and it was distracting beyond measure.

"As far as I'm concerned, I think it would do the family a favor to shred all papers that don't contain pertinent information that would affect our lives today," he said. His voice deepened a notch and he slowed his speech. Was their proximity having an effect on him, too?

Lost in depths of blue, she was mesmerized. Her breath caught and held. He leaned a fraction closer. Her heart raced. With an effort she looked away, trying to get back to their normal relationship. Leaning away from him, she touched the yellowed envelopes in the large box as she tried to get back to his instructions.

"If there is anything about money, boundary rights, water rights, that sort of thing, then place the paper in the box marked Consider and I will read it. If you find maps, drawings, etc., then place them in Miscellaneous."

As what he had told her to do sank in, she frowned. She picked up a tattered, yellow envelope with flowing writing across the front. "This was in the 1800s. Look at the address on it. It's just a name and the county. You want to shred it?"

"If it doesn't have anything pertinent to the matters I listed—rights, boundaries, money. Something significant."

"The letter is significant if it has nothing like that in it. Isn't it written by one of your ancestors?"

"Probably my great-great-grandfather. Maybe further back than that by one generation."

"You can't shred it. It's wonderful to have all these letters from your ancestors and know what they were like," she said, staring at him and wondering how he could care so little about his own family history. "How can you feel that way about them?"

With a smile he shook his head. "It's past and over."

"You have an architectural firm, so you must like old buildings."

"Old buildings are more reliable than people. People change constantly and you can't always count on them. An old building—if it's built right—might last through centuries and you can definitely rely on it."

She stared at him, wondering who had let him down so badly that he would view people as unreliable. Had it started when his mother had walked out on the family? Three young boys. Emma shivered, unable to imagine a mother leaving her young sons. Maybe that was why Zach kept his feelings bottled up. "This is your tie to your past. And your ancestors were reliable or you wouldn't even be here now."

"Okay, so read through the letters. If they're not significant in the manner I've told you, toss them in this basket. Give me two or three of the most interesting and I'll read them and see if I can discover why I should keep them. I think when you get into it, you'll change your mind. I don't want to save letters that tell how the sod roof leaks or the butter churn broke or a wagon needs a new axle."

"I think all those things would be interesting." She tilted

her head to study him. "Family really isn't important to you, is it?"

Shaking his head again, he continued to smile. "Sure it is. I'm close with my brothers. That doesn't mean I want a bunch of old letters none of us will look at twice. They're musty, rotting and of no value." He leaned closer, so close she blinked and forgot the letters. He was only inches away and his mouth was inviting, conjuring up her curiosity about how he kissed.

"You're looking at me as if I just sprouted fangs."

She couldn't get her breath to answer him. His eyes narrowed a tiny fraction and his smile vanished. The look in his eyes changed, intensifying. Her pulse drummed, a steady rhythm that was loud in her ears. "I can't understand your attitude."

"Well, we're alike to a degree there—I can't understand yours," he said lightly. Again a thick silence fell and she couldn't think about letters or the subject of their conversation or even what he had just said. All she thought about was his mouth only a few inches from hers. Realizing the lust-charged moments were happening too often, she shifted and looked away, trying to catch her breath and get back on track.

She stood and stepped away, turning to glance back. "I'll get a pen and paper in case I need to take notes."

"I'll help sort some of these," he said, studying her with a smoldering look.

She wanted to thank him and tell him his help wasn't necessary. It definitely wasn't wanted. She needed to keep space between them. Big spaces. This wasn't a way to start a new assignment. She had no such attraction to men she worked with in Dallas, or anywhere else for that matter. Why was Zach Delaney so compelling?

It was certainly not because he was great fun or because they had so much in common. The only similarities they had were living in Texas at the same time in history and being connected in business to the same company. She had to get a grip on her reactions to him.

In every way he was not the man to be attracted to. Her boss, a world traveler, cared almost nothing for all the things that were important to her, family most of all.

Picking up a tablet, a pen and an empty wooden tray, she returned to her chair, pulling it slightly farther from his, but she couldn't move away because the basket and box to put the old documents in stood between them. She placed the wooden tray on the floor beside her chair.

When she opened the first envelope, a faint, musty odor emanated as she withdrew thin, yellowed pages covered in script. She read the letter from a man who wrote about frontier life, the "beeves" he had rounded up, and his plans to take them north to sell.

"Zach, if this is your great-great-grandfather, you should read this letter and see what kind of life he had," she said impulsively. "It's fascinating. He writes about a wagon train that came through and camped on his land. Is that this same ranch?"

"Same identical one," he remarked dryly, amusement in his expression.

"Listen—'their leader was Samuel Worthington,'" she read. "'Samuel asked if they could stay. He said they had traveled from Virginia and were going west. They had lost four people in their group. The four unfortunates drowned when they crossed a treacherous river after a rain. I gave them flour and beef so they had fresh supplies. Worry ran high about finding water in days to come so I drew Samuel a map of the land I know and showed him where to find water when they left my home. They have great expectations regarding their journey.'"

She lowered the letter to look at Zach. "I think that's wonderful. Don't you feel you know a little now about your great-

great-grandfather? He was kind and generous with those travelers. I would be so excited if these were letters written by my great-great-grandfather."

Zach smiled at her as if facing a bubbling child. "Okay. My great-great-grandfather was a nice guy who was good to people passing through. That knowledge really doesn't bring me closer because he lived years ago. It doesn't change the course of life. He was a rancher in the old days of the longhorns and he had a tough life. He worked hard and was successful and built on the land to pass that on to the next Delaney son. I don't need to wade through all his old letters about life on the plains in the early days."

She tilted her head to study Zach. She was both annoyed by his attitude and at the same time, mesmerized again by his enticing smile. "Do your brothers feel the way you do?"

"We haven't talked about it. I'll ask before I shred these. I would guess that Will might want them and Ryan will feel the same as I do."

She shook her head. "I can't understand your family. You must not have been close growing up."

He shrugged and shook his head. "When our mom walked out and divorced Dad, he sent us away to different boarding schools. I suppose he had some reason that seemed logical to him. We're close in some ways, but we were separated most of the time for a lot of years. It made a difference."

"That's truly dreadful."

He smiled again and her pulse fluttered. "Don't feel too sorry for us. Our father spent a lot of money on us."

"Money doesn't make up for some things."

"We could argue that one all night," he said, leaning back and placing his hands behind his head. The T-shirt stretched tautly across his broad shoulders and his muscles flexed. As he stretched out, she could not keep from taking one swift glance down the length of him. Feathers were holding a dance inside her. Everything quivered and lustful thoughts flashed in her mind. She realized silence was growing again and he watched her with a look of interest. Her mind raced for something, trying to think where the conversation had ended.

"Your great-great-grandfather—I wonder if any of you resemble him."

"You can see for yourself. In the last years of his life, someone painted his portrait. It hangs in the library." He put down his arms and leaned forward. "C'mon. I'll show you."

"You don't need to walk there now. I assume you're supposed to be staying off your foot."

"I can walk around," he said, getting the crutch. "I go to the doc next week and hope to get off this crutch. I'll still be in some kind of crazy medical shoe, but at least I may lose the crutch. C'mon. We'll go look at my old ancestor. I suspect he was a tough old bird. My dad was in his own way. I'm amazed he kept the letters. He didn't have a sentimental bone in his body until the last couple of years of his life. Or maybe since Caroline's birth. That little granddaughter changed him."

"That's family—little children wrap around your heart."

He gave her another big smile. "You're sentimental, Emma."

"I certainly am," she replied cheerfully.

He led the way into the library that held shelves of books from floor to ceiling. A huge portrait in a gilt frame hung above the fireplace and she looked at a stern-faced man with prominent cheekbones, straight gray hair, mustache and beard.

"I can't see that you look like him in any manner at all."

"No, I don't think so either." He gestured across the room. "Over there are portraits of my paternal grandfather and my dad."

She crossed the room. "You don't look like them either."

"If I have a resemblance to any forebears, it's my maternal grandfather. People say I look like him. I don't see it much myself except for the hair. No pictures of him here."

She returned to the fireplace to study the picture, thinking about the letter she had just read. "I'd think you'd want to read every letter in that box."

"I'm leaving that to you."

She turned to find him looking at her intently, a look that was hot and filled with desire, giving her heart palpitations. In spite of his injured foot, he looked strong and fit. Muscled arms, broad shoulders, flat belly. She stepped toward the door.

"We better go back and let me start reading them," she said, heading out of the room, aware that he fell into step beside her. "You said you have brothers. Do they have ranches around here or do all of you gather here?"

"Both. I'm not a rancher, so I've probably spent the least time here, but we were here plenty growing up. Plenty to suit me. I'm not a cowboy and not a rancher and my brothers can ride the horses. No, thanks. Will's ranch adjoins this one. Caroline loves it there, so they go quite often. Ryan's ranch is farther away. He's a cowboy through and through. Maybe it's because he spent too much time out here with Granddad."

"So will your brothers come here this week for Thanksgiving?" she asked, lost in thoughts about her own family's plans. She was taking a corn casserole and a dessert for everyone.

"No. Ryan's with a friend and Will and family are going to his home in Colorado."

"I can't imagine not being with family, but if you're with close friends or a close friend and family, that works," she said, glancing at him to see a grin. "You're staying out here alone, aren't you?" she blurted, aghast to think his brothers were going their own way and Zach had no plans. She started to invite him to her house, but she remembered that her predecessors had not lasted more than a few days at best on this job. If she invited him and then he dismissed her, it would be awkward.

"You're staring, Emma, and you have pity written all over your face," he said. "A new experience in my adult life. I can't remember anyone feeling sorry for me for any reason before."

Heat flushed her cheeks, and she forced a faint smile, hoping the pitying expression would vanish. They had stopped walking and were gazing at each other. He placed a hand on her shoulder lightly. The feathery touch with anyone else would have been impersonal, but with Zach, it was startling.

"It's my choice," he said. "Stop worrying."

"Zach, you can come to our house," she said, changing her mind about inviting him because it was sad to think of him being alone. "My family would be happy to have you. We've always invited friends who would have been alone on Thanksgiving, so I know my family will welcome you."

His grin widened. "Thank you for the very nice invitation, but I rarely notice holidays and don't celebrate them."

"Is this a religious thing?" she asked.

"No. It's a 'my thing.' As I mentioned, my brothers and I grew up in boarding schools, and sometimes we were left there on holidays because our folks were in Europe or heaven knows where," he explained. While he talked, she was acutely conscious of his hand still lightly on her shoulder. His gaze lowered to her lips and she could barely get her breath. It took an effort to pay attention to what he was saying. "None of us care much about holidays. Will is changing because of Caroline and his wife, Ava. I'm usually not in the country on Thanksgiving, but this year spending it alone here on the ranch is what I choose to do. Thank you anyway for your invitation," he said, turning to walk again.

Still physically too aware of him at her side, she strolled beside him. The hot attraction that obviously affected both of them tainted this job. If she got to stay, could she keep their relationship impersonal? She didn't think it would be much of a problem.

This loner, besides being her boss, was not the man to be attracted to. How could he possibly want to spend Thanksgiving alone? Even though he came from enormous wealth, he must have had a cold, lonely childhood. He seemed a solitary person who stayed out of the limelight and worked in distant places where he was unknown. She had seen pictures of his brother in the newspapers and in Texas magazines, but never Zach. He clearly kept a low profile.

As they entered the office, she parted with him and went to her desk to try to concentrate on work.

Over an hour later Zach received a phone call. She continued with her work, but by the time half an hour had passed and he had had three calls, she realized there must be a problem somewhere. He sat with his back to her, his feet propped up on a nearby computer table. The room was large enough that she couldn't hear exactly what he said. When she caught snatches of a few words, she guessed the language was German.

She worked until five to get everything done he had given her. He was still engrossed in phone calls when she shut off her computers and left the room. In her room, she spent over an hour reading and replying to emails from family and close friends before going to the kitchen for dinner.

Thinking of the loner in the office the entire time.

Lowering his feet Zach had swiveled in his chair and watched Emma leave the room, but his many phone calls had demanded his focus. Now, he glanced down at a letter on his desk she had typed. "I'll make the call at 8:00 in the morning your time and see if we can't get this worked out quickly," he said into the phone. "Right, Todd. I'll let you know. It's too late there to call anyone now." He replaced the receiver, glanced at his watch and sighed.

His cell phone indicated a call and he answered because it was Will.

"Can you talk now?" Will asked.

"Yes. We've had problems on a job and I've been on and off the phone for the past two hours."

"I've gotten a busy signal once. How's it going with the new secretary or is it too early to tell?"

Zach glanced again at the letter on the desk. "She's a good secretary. I don't think she'll last though. She's totally wound into her family in Dallas, which is several hours away from here, probably too far. They live, breathe, eat and stay together most of the time."

"Just say the word and I'll get someone else sent out."

"Not yet," Zach said, thinking about Emma's green eyes. "She's efficient. She's sentimental—you'd think these old letters were worth a million the way she views them. She can't keep from telling me I shouldn't shred them."

Will laughed. "Another one telling you what to do?"

"No, not like the first one. Emma's just so into families, she can't understand that I'm not treasuring every word from our ancestor. He was probably a tough old guy, even tougher than Dad. Why would I treasure every word he uttered?"

"You're a little more irreverent than most descendants would be. I'm a little curious about them, so I want to read a few and see what's in those boxes."

"You can have them, Will."

"No. You volunteered. You just need the right secretary to help you. Sounds to me as if you don't have a good fit yet and I should send someone."

"No. She's an excellent secretary. I've piled on the work and she's done it accurately and quickly. I don't want to dump her because she likes the box of old letters."

"True. At least she may really read them."

"Oh, she'll read them all right," Zach said, smiling as he remembered Emma poring over the one, her head bent. Her red hair held gold strands and a healthy shine. She had it pinned up, but strands spilled free and indicated long hair. Long hair and long legs.

"We'll leave in a few weeks for Colorado. If you change your mind and want to come along, or to spend Thanksgiving with us, let me know."

"Thanks, but I'm fine. My new secretary was a little shocked when she learned I'm spending the holiday alone. She invited me to join her family."

There was a moment's pause. "You two are getting to know each other."

"How can we avoid it? Remember, we work all day together and there are just the two of us here except when we see Rosie or Nigel."

"If you were Ryan, I'd ask if she's good-looking, but I've heard you talk too often about avoiding dating employees."

"You and I have agreed that's a complication no one needs in his life. I don't want any part of that kind of trouble," he said, thinking about her full lips and hearing a hollow sound to his words. "There's no need to bring emotions into the workplace—at least the kind of emotions that a relationship would create. Common sense says no way," he added, more to himself than Will.

"It worked with Ava."

"Yeah, but you hired her to work with Caroline—that was different from an office situation and you know it. It's not going to happen here. I get looks from her like I'm from another planet with my feelings about holidays, families and memorabilia."

Will laughed. "I can imagine that one. There are times

you get those looks from me. Ryan is the baby brother and he accepts whatever we do."

"Yeah. I do get those looks from you, but I don't know why because you're like me about sentiment. Or at least you were until Ava and Caroline. Especially Caroline. They've mellowed you until I hardly know you."

"You ought to try it sometime," Will answered lightly. "I'll talk to you before we leave for Colorado."

"Sure, Will. Thanks for the invitation. Tell Ava I said thanks." Zach ended the call and swung his chair around to look out the window without really seeing anything outside. Envisioning Emma, he wanted to be with her again. He had just blown the sensible course. He should have let Will send out another secretary, yet how could he get rid of Emma when her secretarial skills were excellent and she wanted the job? He couldn't send her back because of the steamy chemistry between them.

"Keep it strictly business," he whispered, lecturing himself. Stay away from her except when working. Don't share lunches or dinners or anything else outside of the office and work. Willpower. Resoluteness.

Thinking of the problems on the project in Maine, the buildings the company had bought and intended to replace with one large building, a parking garage and a landscaped area, he tossed down a pen and returned to thinking about Emma. He wanted to have dinner with her, but hadn't he just resolved to avoid her? He didn't want to get involved with an employee, especially a sentimental homebody who could barely leave her family and especially an employee living under the same roof with him. It could complicate his life beyond measure to have her expect some kind of commitment from him and to have rumors flying at the office. He didn't want tears and a scene when he told her goodbye. Thoughts of any of those things gave him chills.

She didn't look like a sentimental homebody, at least his idea of one. Her full red lips, the mass of red hair that was caught up on her head hinted at a wild, party-loving woman. The reactions she had to just a look from him implied a sensuous, responsive lover.

"Damn," he said aloud. Taking a deep breath, he yanked papers in front of him.

Wiping his brow, he leaned over his desk and tried to concentrate on tasks at hand. After two minutes he shoved aside papers and stood. He should send her away, get her out of his life, but the chemistry he wanted to avoid made it impossible to think about giving her up. No matter what he'd just told himself, he wanted to be with Emma—what could a dinner hurt?

With a glance at his watch, he saw he had probably already missed her and a hot dinner from Rosie. Annoyed he would have to eat alone, he headed to the kitchen, hoping Emma was still there.

His disappointment when she wasn't bothered him even more than her absence. Since when had he started to look forward to being with her so much?

Three

The evening was quiet and after dinner Emma stayed in her room. She had eaten alone, experiencing a mix of relief and disappointment that Zach hadn't appeared. It was wiser that he had not eaten with her. The less they socialized, the better, even though there was a part of her that wanted to see him.

On Friday, he appeared wrapped in business and he kept his distance. That afternoon, he told her to leave at one so she could get to Dallas ahead of the traffic.

"Thanks," she replied, smiling broadly. "I'll accept that offer." Shutting down her computer, she was on the road away from the ranch twenty minutes later. They had gotten through the first week, so she must have the job. They also had kept a distance between them. He had been professional, quiet, but there was no way she could feel she had imagined the chemistry simmering just below the surface. Any time they locked gazes, it flared to life, scalding, filled with temptation, an unmistakable attraction.

Now she could believe rumors she had always heard that

he never dated employees, never getting emotionally entangled with anyone on his staff, never even in the most casual way. She intended to keep that professional, remote relationship with him and this job would be a plus on her resume.

If she could just keep from dreaming about him at night—with a sigh, she concentrated on her driving and tried to stop thinking about Zach Delaney. Instead, she reflected on the fun she always had at home with the family and with her nieces and nephews.

Monday when she returned to work, she dressed in jeans, a T-shirt sprinkled with bling, and sneakers. Zach had said jeans were fine and that's what he had worn every workday. Even so, she felt slightly self-conscious when she entered the office.

He was already there and looked up, giving her a thorough glance.

"You said jeans are acceptable," she stated.

"Jeans are great," he said in a tone that conveyed a more personal response. "Yours look terrific," he added, confirming what she thought.

"Thank you," she answered, sitting behind her desk and starting to work.

"This afternoon I'm going to Dallas to see my doctor. Hopefully, I can toss this crutch when I come home."

"You can return to your traveling?"

"How I wish. No. He's already told me that I'll have to wear this and continue to stay off my foot except to get around the house. Still, it'll be an improvement."

"Sure," she replied.

He returned to whatever he had been doing and they worked quietly the rest of the morning. When she left for lunch, he stayed in the office. In the afternoon, she read more Delaney letters, occasionally glancing at the great-great-grandson, continuing to wonder how he could care so little about his history.

The next morning the crutch had disappeared. Zach remained professional and slightly remote. She noticed he hobbled around and kept his foot elevated when he was seated.

On Thursday afternoon she dug inside one of the open boxes of memorabilia and picked up a small box and opened it. Yellowed paper was inside and when she pushed the paper away, she gasped when she discovered a beautiful pocket watch.

"Zach, look at this," she said, turning to take the box to him. He stood by a file cabinet. Today his T-shirt was navy, tight and short-sleeved, revealing firm muscles and a lean, fit body. Dark curls fell on his forehead. As he came around his desk, she handed him the box. Their fingers brushed, sending ripples radiating from the contact.

"This is beautiful," she said. She looked up from the watch, meeting his gaze, ensnared, while tension increased between them. She could barely get her breath. It was obvious he felt something as he focused on her. His attention lowered to her mouth. Her lips parted, tingled while her imagination ran riot. How long before he kissed her?

"Zach," she whispered, intending to break the spell, but she forgot what she had been about to say. He shifted, a slight closing of the space between them. His hand barely touched her waist as he leaned closer. She couldn't keep from glancing at his mouth and then back into crystal blue that held flames of desire.

The air heated, enveloped her, and the moment his mouth touched hers, she closed her eyes. His lips were warm, firm, a dangerous temptation. Her insides knotted, dropping into free fall. Protests vanished before being spoken. Her breath was gone. His lips settled, opened her mouth.

His arm went around her waist tightly, holding her close against his hard body.

She spun away, carried on his kiss. A dream kiss, only it was real, intensifying longing, burning with the impression of a brand that would last. Her hands went to his arms, resting lightly on hard, sculpted muscles.

As his tongue probed and teased, her heart pounded. Passion swamped her caution. She wrapped her arm around his neck and kissed him in return. Standing on tiptoe, she poured herself into her kiss. His arm tightened and he leaned over her, kissing her hard and possessively, making her light-headed. She wound her fingers in his hair as she kissed him, barely aware he was tangling his hand in her own hair.

It was Zach Delaney she kissed wildly. The reminder was dim, but gradually stirred prudence. "Zach," she whispered, looking up at him. Her heart thudded because the look in his eyes scalded, sending its heat to burn her. His mouth was red from kisses, his eyes half closed. His expression held stormy hunger.

"Emma, you like this," he whispered, winding his hand in her hair behind her head, pulling her head closer again.

She wrapped both arms around his neck, holding him and kissing him back. Her heart raced as she gave vent again to desires that had smoldered since she met him.

Their breathing grew harsh while he slipped his hand down her back to her waist.

Again, she grasped at control and raised her head. "I wasn't going to do this."

"I've wanted to since the first minute I saw you," he declared in a rasp. His blue eyes darkened, a sensual, hot look that melted her and made her want to reach for him again.

Instead, she stepped away. "I came over here for a reason," she whispered, unable to get her voice. Her gaze was still locked with his and he looked as surprised as she felt.

His kisses had shaken her. Desire was a white-hot flame. She wanted him in a manner she had never experienced before and the attraction shook her even more than that first day she had met him.

"Zach, I should quit this job right now," she whispered. He gave her a startled look and she could feel her face flush.

"Over a few meaningless kisses?" he asked.

She didn't want to answer him. He stood there looking at her in that sharp manner he had while she struggled to get the right words.

"The kisses—" She paused. She didn't want to admit more to him, but he wanted an answer. "Kisses weren't like others. This was different. We have something—" She waved her hands helplessly.

He inhaled, drawing deeply, his chest expanding as longing flared again in his eyes.

"Common sense tells me to walk away now," she whispered. "You have a reputation for never going out with an employee."

"I never have," he answered. "That doesn't mean I can't."

"That wasn't what I wanted to hear. I want this job."

"We'll do something," he replied, his voice raspy and quiet. "Don't quit. We'll try to stick to work."

She shook her head, looking at his mouth and feeling her pulse speed as they talked. "I can't. I'm quitting. I don't think you need more notice than that. You can find a wonderful, efficient secretary soon enough."

"No," he replied, jamming his hands into his pockets while a muscle worked in his jaw. "I'll double your salary and you stay."

"Double my salary?" she repeated, shaking her head.

"You don't need to pack and go because we kissed. We're adults. If we kiss, it's not that big a deal. There's nothing between us—no history, no ties. If you don't want to get involved, we can both exercise control. With my offer, you'll earn twice as much. Don't walk out on that over a few casual kisses."

Exasperated and stung over his dismissal of kisses that had shaken her, she stared at him. "There's no relationship between us. There's not even any emotional bond. We're practically strangers. But those kisses weren't casual to my way of thinking," she whispered.

She stepped close, put her arm around his neck and placed her mouth on his, kissing him with all the heat and fury she felt over his dismissive attitude. After one second that probably was his surprise holding him immobile, his arm banded her waist and he returned her kiss. Fully. He pressed against her, his tongue going deep while she kissed him, trying to set him on fire. In seconds she broke off the kiss and looked up with satisfaction.

"I'd say your body's reaction isn't casual."

With his eyes darkened, his breathing was ragged. She had felt the hard throb of manhood against her and his heart pounding.

"Okay. Kisses damn well aren't casual, but I'm trying to get us back there," he said. A muscle worked in his jaw. When his attention focused on her mouth, she stepped back.

"Do you still want to double my salary—or do you want me to go?"

"I'll double your salary," he replied, grinding out the words.

"You'll double my salary to get me to continue as your secretary. You know I can't turn that down."

"I hope not. You're a good secretary," he answered in a more normal tone of voice.

Inhaling deeply, she promised herself she would exercise better control.

"Against good judgment, I'll stay. I can't say no. I need the money for my college plans."

"That's settled." They stared at each other until she realized what she was doing.

"I came over here for something," she said, feeling foolish, struggling against stepping into his arms again, yet determined to regain her composure. She looked around and spotted the small box on the corner of Zach's desk. She retrieved the box, clinging to it as if it were a lifeline.

"Look at this."

He was still gazing at her and his blue eyes had darkened again. His expression no longer appeared as impersonal. Her heart drummed while her lips tingled. The urge to reach for him tormented her. With a deep breath he looked down, picked up the watch and turned it in his hand.

"This is a find," he said, his voice deep, becoming hoarse, and she was certain the husky tone was not caused by the watch he held. "This watch is worth going through the box of stuff." Turning it in his hand, he studied the gold back. "These are my great-great-grandfather's initials," Zach said, extending it to her and she looked down, stepping closer to gaze at the watch, which she had already studied. "Warner Irwin Delaney," Zach read. "This we'll keep, thank you, Emma."

"It's a beautiful pocket watch. I'm glad you're keeping it. I'll research to find one like it to pinpoint how old it is. For the moment, I'll see what else I can find."

"I'll help for a while," he said. "The watch makes poking around in all the old stuff more interesting."

She returned to her chair, mindful of him pulling one up nearby. The awareness of him was sharp, intense and disturbed her concentration. She wanted to take a long look at him, but she didn't want to get caught studying him.

She tried to focus on a letter and realized her concentration was on Zach only. His kisses had been fantastic, setting her on fire in a blaze that still burned. She wanted more kisses, wanted to dance and flirt and make love—reactions that shocked her. Ones she had never experienced before in this manner. The men in her life had always been friends, family-oriented guys she had been comfortable with. Never anyone she had been very serious about either. Why did he hold such appeal for her?

She could barely think about the jump in salary for thinking about the man. Any other time in her life she would have been overjoyed at the increase in pay, but now it kept slipping her mind, replaced by thoughts about Zach.

The wise thing to do would be to pack and go no matter what salary he offered. She couldn't do it. The salary was important. College—and her classes on the internet—was expensive. This boost in salary filled a great need. Without thinking, she glanced at him. He was studying her openly and she felt her face flush as they looked into each other's eyes.

The glance had the same effect as a touch.

They worked in silence. As he methodically shoved aside letters, she realized he was looking for more things like the watch. She became absorbed in her reading.

"I feel as if I know part of your family," she said, folding a letter. "After the Civil War, Warner Delaney started building this ranch house. He brought his family out here. Earlier, he met a woman in Kansas City and is going to ask her to marry him."

"My great-great-grandmother? Her name was Tabitha, I think."

They heard a commotion in the hall and a tall man in Western boots, jeans, a navy sweater and a Stetson entered the room. He held the hand of a little black-haired girl who smiled broadly at Zach and then glanced shyly at Emma.

"Will. Caroline. How's my prettiest and favorite niece?" Zach asked, lifting her up and holding her to kiss her cheek.

She laughed and giggled as he set her on her feet. "Hey, Will. Where's Ava?"

"Stopped to talk to Rosie and leave Muffy with her. Muffy is a dog," he explained, glancing at Emma.

"Emma, this is my niece, Caroline, and my brother Will Delaney. Ah, here is Ava. Emma, meet Ava Delaney. This is Emma Hillman, my secretary."

As she shook hands with the adults, Emma gazed into warm welcoming green eyes of a sandy-haired blonde. Caroline, holding a small brown bear, could not stop smiling.

"C'mon, let's go into the family room where it's more comfortable and Caroline has things to play with while we talk," Zach suggested.

Will smiled. "We were on our way back from Dallas and stopped for a few minutes to see about you."

"Zach, all of you go ahead," Emma said. "I can stay in here. I don't want to intrude—"

"C'mon, Emma, or we'll all have to sit in here on these hard chairs," Zach said with a shake of his head.

"Please join us," Ava said. "Don't leave Caroline and me alone with these two."

Emma smiled and nodded, knowing Ava was teasing and it was nice that they would include her. Will was strikingly handsome without the ruggedness of Zach. She would not have picked them out of a crowd as brothers because Will's dark eyes were nothing like Zach's vivid blue ones. Their facial structure was as different as their hair.

"Well, the offer is still open for you to have Thanksgiving with us," Will said.

"Thanks. I'll still stay here. You know Rosie will cook a big turkey."

"You should join us, Zach," Ava said. "The snow will be beautiful and we'll have a great time."

"Thanks, Ava. I'll do fine here," he replied without glancing at Emma.

When they entered the family room, Emma mulled over his turning down the offer for Thanksgiving. How could he turn down Will and stay alone on the isolated ranch? She would never understand how Zach could possibly avoid being lonely and miserable. Was this all a carryover from childhood hurts, seeking isolation because it was a shield against times he had been left alone and deeply disappointed?

"So how are you doing with the memorabilia?" Will asked.

"I want to show you what Emma found in that box of old letters. I'll put it with anything else of value we find."

"I'll get it," Emma said. "You talk to your family." Before Zach could protest she hurried from the room. In minutes she returned to hand the box to Zach.

As she sat down, he took the watch and held it up. "Look at this."

"That looks like a fine watch and something nice to keep since it belonged to a Delaney ancestor," Will said. Zach carried it to show it to Ava and Caroline who crowded around them. Will got up to join them.

"If this isn't just like Dad," Zach said. "I'll bet he found the watch and stuck it back in with the letters to let us find it."

"I don't know. I had the feeling he had never gone through that stuff before," Will remarked.

"Maybe not. No telling what else I'll find. Or Emma will find."

"I hear you're the one reading the letters," Will said, smiling at her.

"Yes, most of them."

"She's far more interested and views them as sacred chunks of our family history and Texas history, but I don't have quite the same respect for them."

The men returned to their seats and Zach placed the watch in the box on a table.

Emma's mystification about Zach's solitary way of life grew as she listened to the brothers and realized they were close and enjoyed each other's company. And Zach was good with Caroline. When Caroline walked over to him, he lifted her to his lap and focused his attention on her.

Shortly she climbed down and went to get into Will's lap and turn his face so he looked at her. She whispered in his ear.

"Yes, we will right now," Will said, looking at Zach. "Caroline has some family news to tell you."

Caroline couldn't sit still and had a big smile. She climbed down and ran to Zach to stand at his knee. She gave another shy glance at Emma and Emma suddenly suspected she was interrupting a family moment. She wanted to leave them to themselves, but she was afraid that would be even more disruptive, so she sat quietly.

Caroline's big smile broadened. "Uncle Zach, I'm going to become a big sister."

"You are!" Zach looked over her head at his brother. "Congratulations!"

"It's early, but we told Caroline because we want to do some remodeling and build a nursery, not only in Dallas, but at my ranch here and in Colorado."

"That is great news, Caroline," Zach said. "Wow! You'll be a big sister and I'll be an uncle again."

She laughed and turned in a circle.

Zach crossed the room to hug Ava lightly. "Congratulations. That's wonderful."

"We think so," she said, her eyes sparkling. She looked radiant as she glanced at her husband and exchanged a look with him. They were obviously so much in love Emma felt slightly envious. Ava reached out to hug Caroline and Will picked her up, holding her while she wrapped her arm around his neck. "We're thrilled," Ava added.

"Congratulations to all of you," Emma said. "You have wonderful news." She looked at Caroline. "Caroline, you'll have lots of fun with your little brother or sister."

Caroline nodded and smiled.

"We're excited," Will said. "And we'll let you both go back to work. We need to get to the ranch. Caroline has been promised to get to ride her horse."

"It's been nice to meet you," Ava said to Emma. "We're glad you're working here. Zach needs help with all the old papers."

"Just keep him from shredding them," Will remarked dryly.

"I find them fascinating," Emma said. "I'm beginning to feel as if I knew Warner Delaney. It was so nice to meet all three of you and it was good of you to include me in your family moment."

"Do you think my unsentimental brother would care who he shares family news with?" Will remarked dryly, grinning at Zach.

As they left the room, Emma stayed back and returned to her desk. She didn't go back to work, but sat staring into space, thinking about Zach. What a waste of someone's life to take away the fabulous moments shared with family and friends. How could he turn down Ava's invitation to spend Thanksgiving with Will and his family? Instead, he would sit in isolation at home on the ranch—a sad choice.

She sat by the box to read a letter, finally concentrating on her work.

When Zach returned, her pulse jumped. He was off-limits, a danger to her peace of mind because her volatile reactions to him had not dwindled even a degree.

"I enjoyed meeting your family. They're great and that's fantastic news they shared."

"My brother amazes me. He'd been as opposed to marriage as any of us, yet he is so in love with Ava, it's ridiculous. And he's great with Caroline. None of us have ever been around children and to become her guardian was really tough for him."

"Well, from what little I saw, Caroline is a very happy little girl."

"Ava and Will have been terrific for her. Ava was the one who suggested Muffy, a little puff of a dog that brought Caroline out of her grief from losing her father more than anything or anybody else."

"Did I hear her call him 'Daddy Two'?"

He nodded. "We've gotten used to that. Will is her second dad since her blood father died and I think she wanted a mom and dad. You noticed she calls Ava Mom?"

"Yes, I did. They seem incredibly happy. How could you not want to be with them for Thanksgiving?"

"I'm my own company. I get along fine."

She shook her head. "Amazing," she said, reaching for another letter. "Do all of you get together for Christmas?"

He gave her a lazy smile and she guessed his answer. As shocked as she was over Thanksgiving, her surprise was greater this time. "You're spending Christmas here alone? You can't do that."

"Of course I can," he replied with laughter in his voice.

"I'd think all of you would gather here since this is the family ranch. Isn't this where you had Christmas celebrations when you were growing up?"

"Maybe twice when Granddad lived here. Never, after he was gone. My mother hated the ranch. Any ranch. If we celebrated together, it was in Dallas. After Mom walked, we didn't even come home for Christmas."

"Zach—"

His jaw firmed and an eyebrow arched. She realized she should stop talking about his personal life. She shrugged and turned away, going back to work without saying anything else. He did the same and she fought the urge to stare at him. How could he spend Christmas all alone? She couldn't imagine anyone doing that through choice.

They worked for the next hour and Zach stood, stretching again.

"Enough of this," he said. "Let's break. I'll go lift weights and do what I can do without involving my foot. We have treadmills or the track. Or an exercise bicycle. Nigel will be there because if any of us lift weights, he appears. He doesn't want us alone if we're working out with weights. That's a long-standing rule and he walks around the track, which is probably good for him. If you prefer, you can sit in the family room and have a lemonade or a cup of hot tea or anything else you want."

"Enough choices," she said, putting down a letter. "I'll change quickly and get on a treadmill. I'd rather sit on the terrace after work."

"Good enough. See you in the gym."

She left him, hurrying upstairs to change.

If only Zach felt about holidays the way Nigel felt about working out. That one shouldn't go it alone.

With Nigel walking on the indoor track, Zach hoisted a bar, lifting it high and lowering it slowly when he saw Emma enter the gym. He set the bar in place and wiped his forehead with a towel while watching her. She wore blue shorts and a blue T-shirt that revealed lush curves, a tiny waist and heart-stopping long legs.

She smiled and waved, going to a treadmill to start it.

He should have let her go back to Dallas. She was a great

secretary, as well as pure trouble. Their kisses were dynamite and the last kiss—when she wanted to prove their kisses couldn't be called casual—had ignited fires that still blazed. Her sudden kiss had shocked and electrified him. It had been a spunky, devil-may-care, I'll-show-you challenge that he would never have expected from her. If he could have burned to cinders from a kiss, he would have with that one. His reaction had definitely not been casual and she knew it. She had more than proven her point. She had driven it home with a wrecking ball.

She had a backbone and he suspected she was as strong-willed as he. Not his kind of woman in any manner except physically. She had been aghast over his plans for a solitary Christmas. He would bet the ranch he hadn't heard the last on that one. She would want to take him home with her for Christmas. The whole thing would be humorous and he could ignore it easily, except she was getting to him in a manner he hadn't thought possible. The hot kisses he had labeled "casual" blasted his peaceful life with constant fantasies about holding her and making love to her.

He wasn't concentrating well on his work. It took real effort to avoid eating lunch or dinner with her. He had offered this exercise time when he should have left the office, worked out with only Nigel and let her continue with her secretarial duties. Common sense said to either practice more self-control or get rid of her.

His lusty body just wanted to seduce her.

Frustrated, he returned to working out.

At one point he paused, glancing over to see Emma running on the treadmill. She was going at good clip, had an easy stride and looked as if she had done this before. She looked fit and tempting. The T-shirt clung, the blue darker where it was damp with perspiration. She had a sexy bounce as she ran and her long legs were as shapely as he had imagined.

With a groan, he returned to his weights. When he stopped, she had finished and had a towel around her neck as she stood talking to Nigel. He smiled, glancing at Zach who waved Nigel away as a signal he was leaving the gym. Since Zach was finished, Nigel headed for the door and, without a glance, Emma followed close behind.

Zach hung behind. He hobbled out of the gym, wanting his foot to heal so he could get back to normal. He went to shower, wrapping his foot in a plastic boot and keeping it out of the shower to avoid getting it wet.

He constantly thought about taking her out when his foot healed and taking her to bed even sooner. If he didn't want to complicate his life, that would not happen. She definitely would have her heart in an affair, something he had always avoided. In spite of what he knew he should refrain from doing, he could not keep from wanting to be with her and fantasizing about it.

Heat climbed, erotic images of Emma in his arms tormenting him. She was getting to him in ways no other woman ever had. So far, her resistance had been almost nil until he offered to double her salary. He suspected they both had acted impulsively. He couldn't bear the thought of losing his excellent secretary and to be truthful to himself, he just didn't want her to go out of his life yet. She hadn't been able to resist because she was trying to save money to finish her college courses. Had part of her wanted to stay because of the attraction?

Out of the shower, he decided not to go back to the office. He could work somewhere else in the house the rest of the day and keep space between them.

He ate dinner alone as he had most nights of his adult life. He had had affairs, but they had usually been brief, casual, on-and-off relationships. His job added to his solitary life. Tonight, he was restless, still drowning in thoughts of Emma. Finally, he had enough of his own company and went to look for her, hoping she had not shut herself in her room for the night.

But she had. He had to remember it was for the best.

Four

Monday, they returned to their regular work routine. Late that day local meteorologists began to warn of a large, early storm from the west predicted to reach Texas on Thursday or Friday. Each day they checked the weather, Emma surprised that Zach ate lunch and dinner with her, flirting, friendly and heightening desire with every encounter.

By Thursday, pictures were coming in from the west of all the snow. "We're ready for the storm, here at the ranch," Zach told Emma. "We have supplies of every sort and enough food for weeks. I think you're stuck, Emma, unless you want to take off work and head to Dallas this afternoon." They both listened as the TV weatherman showed a massive storm dumping twelve inches of snow in the mountains in New Mexico and blanketing Interstate 40, closing it down.

"Now they're predicting it'll come in here Friday," Zach repeated. "If you beat the storm home, you'll be stuck there, which is fine if you want to do that."

"I can miss one weekend at home," she said. "Actually, I

can go ahead and work and get more of the letters read and go through things."

"If you're sure. I've told Nigel and Rosie the same thing. Rosie's cooking up a storm herself, but if we get what they're predicting, neither of them will come in. I've told them to stay home."

"I'll stay here, Zach. I don't want to get caught in bad weather. From what they're predicting, it will come and go and be clear for me to go home for Thanksgiving next week."

"If you decide to stay, I'll pay you overtime."

"That isn't necessary. I'm happy to be out of the storm. Mom's already called worrying about me."

"Call her so she can stop worrying."

"Thanks, Zach."

"I wish I could take you out dancing Saturday night, but that's out because of the storm and my foot. We can have a steak dinner—I'll cook. We can have our own party here."

She laughed. "Sounds great, but you don't have to do that."

His blue eyes held a lusty darkness and his voice lowered. "I want to. Even though it might not be the wisest thing for either one of us, a cozy evening in front of a fire while it snows outside sounds fun. Now I can't wait for the first flakes to fall."

Shaking her head, she smiled at him while her insides fluttered. Saturday night with Zach would not be the same as working together in a spacious office. "In the meantime, let's go back to work," she said, pulling her chair close to the open box of letters.

She read more letters—some were by his great-grandfather, most by his great-great-grandfather, all of them mixed together. She had trays she would place them in according to generation. She had made trays labeled by dates, water rights, and "boundary disputes." She tried to sort them all the ways that would be helpful. If she had time before the job ended, she would put them in chronological order.

She had read five letters when she shoved her hand into the box to get more and felt a hard lump beneath the letters. She moved them carefully, placing them to one side in the box, and found two objects wrapped in cloth. "Zach, there are some things in this box. They're wrapped in rags." She carefully continued to remove letters as he crossed the room. He bent over to plunge his hand in.

"Zach, be careful with the letters."

"Ah, Emma, these letters are not priceless heirlooms."

"They may be to some of your family."

"I'll be damned," he said, grasping something wrapped in cloth and pulling it out of the box. He tossed away the rags. "This is a Colt. It's a beauty." He checked to see if it was loaded—it wasn't. "This is fantastic. You said there were two things."

He placed the Colt on an empty chair and turned to reach into the box to withdraw the other object wrapped in cloth.

"It's a rifle," he said, unwrapping strips of rags that had yellowed with age. Zach tossed them into a trash basket and held the rifle in his hands, checking to be certain it was not loaded. "It's a Henry. I'll say my ancestors knew their weapons. A Colt revolver and a Henry rifle." He raised it to aim toward the patio. "This is a find. Why would anyone stick these in with a bunch of letters? If I had been the only descendant, I would have pitched the boxes and never given them another thought."

"Well, aren't we all glad keeping the heirlooms was not left to you alone," she said sweetly and he grinned.

"The Henry was a repeating rifle that came out about the time the Civil War began. This is fabulous," he said, running his hand over it. "Now I can feel a tie with my ancestors with these two weapons. Ryan is going to love both of these. So will Will."

"You make it sound as if all of you are gun-toting cowboys, which I know is not the case. Far from it. You're a man of cities."

"I still love this. It's a beaut and Will and Ryan are going to love it. Garrett—he's a family friend—won't be so wound up over it, I don't think. He's the city person, which makes it funny that Dad willed this ranch to Garrett and not to any of his sons. It's also why Garrett is in no rush to claim it. This Henry is something."

She picked up an envelope. "If you'll excuse me, you can go drool over your guns while I read." She withdrew a letter. "Want me to read aloud?"

"I don't think so, thank you," he said, smiling. He picked up the revolver and carried a weapon in each hand back to place them on his desk. As soon as he sat, he called Will to tell him about the latest find.

They talked at length before he told Will goodbye and then called Ryan to tell him about the revolver and the rifle. She shook her head and bent over the latest letter, still thinking the letters were the real treasure.

It was an hour before he finished talking to both brothers. With his hands on his hips, he looked at the boxes. "Some of the boxes have objects of value. There's one more box. I wonder if each one will hold its own treasure. I'll start looking through this box," he said, sitting down and pulling a box close. He took out a bunch of letters and put them on the floor.

"These letters are not packed away in any apparent order," she said. "Put the letters in this box because it's almost empty now. You'll tear them up, dumping them out like that. I'll help you."

"The precious letters. I'll take more care," he said, and began to shift them to the box she had beside her. When his box was three-fourths empty, hers had been filled. He bent over his box and felt around. "I don't feel anything, except letters."

"Try reading a few," she suggested.

He frowned slightly and picked up a letter to skim over it. "Nothing," he said, tossing it into the discard box and taking another. After an hour, Zach was clearly tired of his fruitless search. "I can't find anything worth keeping."

"Maybe I *should* get in the car and go home now. It's sort of tempting fate to stay."

"You made a decision to stay. If you were going you should have left hours ago. You made your decision, so stick with it. If you leave now, you could get caught if the storm comes in early. You'd be in the snow in the dark. Not a good combination. Just stay."

Stay, she'd have to.

On Friday the storm arrived as predicted, the first big flakes falling late morning. Emma went to the window. "Zach, this is beautiful. I have to go outside to look." She left the office and went out the back to the patio to stand and watch huge flakes swirling and tumbling to earth. She stuck out her tongue, letting an icy flake melt in her mouth. She also held up her palm, watching for the briefest second as a beautiful flake hit her and then transformed into a drop of icy water.

In seconds she heard the door and glanced around to see Zach hurrying outside with a blanket tossed around his shoulders.

"I thought you might be cold," he said, shaking it so it was around her and over her head as well as covering him. With his arm around her shoulders, he held the blanket in place. Shivering, she pressed closer, relishing the cozy warmth of Zach beside her.

"Isn't this beautiful! I love the snow. It would be fun to have a white Christmas if it didn't keep people from their families."

"Your family will probably build snow forts and snowmen this weekend."

She smiled. "Our yard will be filled with snow sculptures, bunnies, snow dogs, forts, tons of snowballs, snowmen. Our local paper came out one year and took pictures. We have sleds and everyone will go sledding if they can."

"I guess in their own way, your family really enjoys life."

"In the best way possible, they enjoy life," she said, looking up at him. "Okay, I'm ready to go back in." She tossed the blanket over his shoulder and dashed for the back door, feeling her cascade of hair swing as she ran.

Inside she stomped her feet to get the snow off and wiped her shoes on the mat. Zach appeared and did the same, best he could with his still-injured foot. "Want coffee, tea or hot chocolate to take back to the office?"

"Sure, hot chocolate."

In minutes she had a mug and was at her desk, concentrating on work and trying to forget about Zach and how he had looked with big snowflakes in his thick brown hair and on his eyelashes.

"Emma," Zach interrupted her during the afternoon. "Look outside now."

She had been concentrating on work and forgotten the snow. The wind had picked up and when she glanced out, she gasped.

Snow was "falling" horizontally and the entire world was white. Everything in sight was buried in snow except the tall trees that were dark shadows as a blizzard raged.

"I didn't notice. Oh, my word. I'm glad I didn't get caught out in that." She walked to the window and heard him coming to join her. Once again he draped his arm lightly across her shoulders.

"Tomorrow night, we'll have our fancy steak dinners. Tonight it will be informal and cozy with Rosie's Texas chili and homemade tamales. We can curl up by the fire and watch a movie or play chess or whatever you want to do. I can think of a few other possibilities," he added in a huskier tone.

"Chess and a movie sound perfect. Forget the other possibilities. Stop flirting."

"We'll see what the evening brings," he said, caressing her arm lightly. "And at the moment, I can't resist flirting."

"Try," she said, taking a deep breath. She looked outside again, shivering just because the storm looked icy and hazardous. Once again she was thankful she wasn't traveling. "I'm glad Rosie and Nigel are off. No one should be out in this. What about your livestock?"

"That's who is out there fighting the elements and working—the cowboys who take care of that livestock at times like this. Just hope there's nothing unusual happening with any of the stock."

She nodded. "I'll go back to work. I've received a text from Mom and all my family is home now except those who work close and they'll be home soon. Some businesses have closed early."

"Our Dallas office closed two hours ago. I have a policy with my CEO and with the vice presidents—whoever is in charge when I'm away—I don't want anyone caught in this getting home. They've all had time to go home."

"That's nice, Zach," she said as she returned to her desk.

They worked until five when Zach stood and stretched. "Time to quit, Emma. Actually past time to stop."

"We're out of the storm and I don't mind continuing."

"I mind. Come on—knock off and we'll meet back down here for a drink and then dinner. Want to meet here at six?"

"Sure," she said, shutting down her computer while he turned and left the room. She closed up and went to her room to shower and change. Dressing in a bright red sweater and matching slacks, she brushed her hair and tied it behind her head with a scarf.

Eagerly, she went downstairs to search for him. She followed enticing smells to the kitchen and found Zach stirring a steaming pot. He put the lid back in place. The minute she saw him, she forgot dinner. He wore a bulky navy sweater that made his shoulders appear broader than ever, and faded jeans that emphasized his narrow hips and long legs. He was in the health shoe and his loafer. Tangled curls were in their usual disarray. Zach's eyes drifted slowly over her, an intense study that had the same results as a caress. Then his gaze locked with hers and her mouth went dry. She was held mesmerized while her heart became a drumbeat that she was certain he could hear. Captured by his look, she remained still while he stopped stirring and set aside the spoon to saunter toward her.

Her heart thudded as she tingled in a growing temptation. "Zach," she whispered, uncertain if she protested or invited because she wanted to do both.

He reached for her, drawing her to him to kiss her.

Her stomach lurched while longing blazed. His passionate kiss demanded her response. Trembling, she returned his kisses, her tongue stroking his and going deep, exploring and tasting. He smelled of mint and deep woods. His lean body was hard planes against her softness, building her excitement.

Zach reached beneath her sweater, sliding his hand up to flick free her bra and then cup her breast as his thumb stroked her. Pleasure fluttered over her nerves and tickled her insides while she clung tightly to him. Finally, she looked up at him.

"Zach, this is exactly what I intended to avoid."

"So did I," he whispered. "It's impossible. Just plain, downright impossible," he added before kissing her.

Moaning with pleasure again, she twisted against him. He was aroused, ready to love. He unfastened her slacks, pushing them off, and they tumbled around her ankles. Kicking off her shoes, she stepped out of them.

Tearing herself away from his kiss, she gasped. "Zach, we're crossing a line."

"I told you, we crossed that line the day you walked into my office for this job. This was inevitable."

"So ill matched and not what I want," she said, looking into eyes that had darkened to a cobalt blue. "A total disaster."

"You want this with all your being. You can't stop," he whispered. His mouth ended her argument. Knowing he was right, she wanted him and she wasn't inclined to stop. She kissed him even though she'd declared their lovemaking a disaster and meant every word.

With deliberation he held her away to look at her and she stepped out of her pooled slacks. He pulled free her red sweater and her unfastened lacy bra went with it. His seductive gaze inched slowly over her, made her pulse race.

"You're beautiful," he whispered, caressing her breasts. Pausing, he tossed away his sweater and she inhaled deeply at the sight of his chest that tapered to a flat washboard belly ridged with muscles.

His hands rested on her hips as his gaze dallied over her, taking in the sight with measured thoroughness. "You're gorgeous," he whispered hoarsely. "You take my breath."

She tingled beneath his sensual perusal. Wherever his gaze drifted, she reacted as if it were his fingers instead of eyes that trailed over her.

He untied her hair, pulling loose the delicate silk scarf, letting the free end slip down in a feathery whisper over her breast before he let go and the scarf fluttered away.

"Your hair is meant for a man's fingers. I've thought that since I saw you get out of your car the first day."

"Zach," she whispered, shaking with need as she reached to pull him close. He resisted, catching her hands, finishing his study. Caresses followed with his fingers touching where he had looked.

"Zach," she gasped, closing her eyes, trembling when she reached for him. He held her away, continuing his sweet torment. His feather strokes started at her throat, moving to her nape and down her back, up her side and then over her breasts, lingering, circling a taut point with his palm. She inhaled and moaned. "Zach," she protested, tugging on his waist because she wanted to press against him and kiss him, to caress him. "We shouldn't kiss."

"Neither of us wants to stop. You want this and I want you. We've been headed for this moment from the first. Ah, Emma," he whispered. His fingers slid over her belly, drawing light circles that tormented and heightened desire.

She throbbed with need. Hunger to love him built swiftly. His fingers slipped up the inside of her thigh and she gasped, spreading her legs. Then he caressed her intimately. Her heart pounded and her eyes flew open as she pulled him roughly to her and kissed him, pouring out her need.

With shaking fingers, she unfastened his belt and then his jeans, shoving them off.

"Your foot?"

"It's protected by the shoe. Ignore it." He yanked off his loafer and then his briefs followed.

She drew a deep breath at the sight of him.

His arms held her tightly. His rock-hard muscles pressed against her while his manhood thrust insistently. He picked her up to carry her in front of the fire, lowering her to an area rug. Flames warmed her side, but she barely noticed for looking into hungry blue eyes.

"You're beautiful." Kneeling, he showered kisses on her. She couldn't stop. Couldn't tell him no. A disaster was blowing in with the storm that raged outside. His hands strummed over her, building need. Her pulse thundered in her ears as she wrapped her arms around his neck, wanting to devour him.

As his hands stroked her, her hips arched to meet him. She wanted more, had to have his hands on her. He stretched out beside her, turning her into his arms while he kissed her and his hand stroked her thighs, moving between them to heighten her pleasure.

"Zach," she breathed, sitting up and leaning over him. She trailed her fingers over the hard muscles, tangling her hand in his chest hair, showering kisses on his shoulder and down over his chest to his belly, moving lower.

As she kissed and caressed him, Zach combed his fingers through her hair. In minutes he sat up to roll her over while he kissed her.

"Zach, I'm not protected," she whispered.

"I'll be right back," he whispered, his tongue trailing over the curve of her ear, stirring waves of sensation while his hand drifted down over her. He rolled away and stood, crossing to get something from the pocket of his jeans and return. He came down to hold her and kiss her, loving her until once again she thrashed beneath him.

Kneeling between her legs, he picked up a packet he had laid aside earlier. She drank in the sight of him while her heart thudded with longing. She had gone beyond the point of saying no, caught up in passion, wanting him.

Stroking his thighs, rough brown curls were an erotic sensation against her palms. He lowered himself, kissing her. His tongue went deep into her mouth, stroking her while she returned his kiss and clung to him. He eased into her, pausing, driving her to a desperate need as he thrust slowly.

Her pounding heart deafened her. Consumed by passion, she wanted him, longed to give herself to him. She had shut off thought earlier and was steeped in sensation, knowing only Zach's body and his loving.

She arched, moaning, crying out until his mouth covered hers again and his kiss muffled sounds she made.

Zach maintained control. Sweat beaded his brow as he continued to thrust slowly. Dimly, she was aware he held back to heighten her pleasure, a sensual torment that made her want more. Urgency tore at her. As she clung tightly to him, beneath her desire ran a current of awareness that she bonded with Zach during this snowy night. This would be a forever event, always in her memory, burning deeply into her life no matter what he felt.

She tossed wildly beneath him until his control vanished. Zach pumped frantically, thrusting deep, his hips moving swiftly.

She arched, stiffened and cried out, her hips moving while ecstasy burst over her, showering her with release.

He shuddered while she clung to him, moving with him, for once both of them, in this moment, well matched. Maybe the only such time. Rapture spread in every vein, running in streams of satisfaction. Sex was breathtaking, incredible, earthshaking in her world.

She could no longer turn back time or erase the occasion. Zach had just become a facet of her life. He could disappear tomorrow, but this night had happened.

"How did we get here?" she whispered, stroking damp curls off his forehead.

"We walked in here with our eyes open. We're where we both wanted to be. You can't deny that."

She kissed his shoulder lightly. "No, I can't," she said, smiling at him and winding her arms around his neck. Tonight she had made him significant in her life, something she shouldn't have done.

"I think it's the perfect place to be," he said, combing long strands of her hair away from her face. "Snow outside, cozy and warm in here, you in my arms, wild lusty love. Totally gorgeous. Best sex ever. I couldn't ask for anything more."

"At the moment, I have to agree."

"For the first time, I'm glad I hurt my foot. Otherwise, our paths would have never crossed. If I had passed you in the Dallas office, I would have noticed you, but I wouldn't have gotten to know you. Not unless you had become my secretary there."

"Not likely. This Friday night hasn't gone according to plan."

"It definitely changed for the better," he whispered, showering kisses on her face and caressing her. "How about a hot tub together?"

"I think that's a great suggestion, but I thought you had to keep your foot out of water."

"I do. I've gotten very adept at hanging my foot out of the shower. I'm sure I can prop it on the edge of the tub."

"You can't hop into a tub," she said, laughing.

He laughed and stood, scooping her into his arms. "I'll carry you to a hot shower instead."

"No," she said, alarmed. "Zach, put me down. You'll hurt your foot."

"Nonsense. I carried you earlier and I didn't hear a protest. We'll do it this time the same way," he said, kissing her and ending her argument.

Carrying her to a bedroom with an adjoining shower, he set her down. He had to give up showering together. As soon as they returned to bed, he pulled her into his embrace to kiss her.

Past midnight Zach held her close. "Ready now for some of Rosie's chili?"

Emma stretched lazily, kissed his cheek and smiled at him. "I think I've lost my appetite."

"I've found mine. Let's go and when you smell it, you'll probably want some. Want a glass of wine or one of my margaritas first?"

"Seems like this is the way we started the evening," she said, wrapped in contentment. She suspected she had already complicated her life and she refused to worry about it on a wonderful night that had turned special. Tomorrow's worries would come soon enough.

"I think you're right."

He stepped out of bed, went to a closet and returned wearing a navy robe. He handed her a dark brown robe. "For you, although I definitely prefer you without it."

"No way, for dinner."

Zach placed his arm around her shoulders as they walked to the kitchen.

"The chili has cooked on low all evening, so it's ready," he said, getting out a covered dish. "I'll get our margaritas, build a fire and we'll eat when we're ready."

In minutes he had drinks mixed and logs stacked to get a fire blazing. He turned out the lights, leaving just firelight and the snowy view outside.

She walked to the window. "Zach, it looks even more beautiful than earlier today. Tomorrow morning we have to build a snowman if it's wet snow."

"Don't count on it. This is a cold night outside. It couldn't be hotter in here," he added in a husky voice.

She smiled at him. "When did you last build a snowman?"

"Probably when I was five. I don't remember exactly, but we did when we were little. A bunch of little boys—of course, we did."

She smiled and he walked to her, carrying their drinks.

"Here's to the very best night ever."

Surprised, she touched his glass with hers. "I'll drink to that and I agree," she said. She sipped the margarita and looked at the snow. "It's beautiful out there, but I'm ready to sit by the fire."

"In front of the fire is much cozier than here by cold windows."

Tossing a bunch of pillows from the sofa to the floor in front of the fire, he held out his arm. "Come here and enjoy the warmth."

She sat on the floor and he drew her back against him. "This is great, Zach."

He curled a lock of her hair in his fingers. "When do you plan to go back to college?"

"I'm saving money and this job helps. I hope to start again next September. I'll take night or Saturday classes or on the computer."

"You can't just take a year off to go back to college?"

"I like my job at your office. I hate to leave it."

"I can promise you it'll be there if you want to come back."

She smiled at him. "Thanks, but I probably need the income, too. I don't think I can save that much."

"Do you have to get presents for that enormous family of yours?"

"The adults draw names. We all give to Mom and Dad. Right now we don't draw names for the kids because there aren't that many and they're little, so they're easy, but I expect the year to come when they do draw kids' names. Our family is growing and two of us are still single."

He took her drink and placed it on the table. One look in his eyes and her pulse jumped while he drew her to him.

"Zach," she said with longing. Sliding her hands over his muscled shoulders, she wrapped her arms around him to kiss him as he pulled her down on the pillows.

Hours later Zach emerged from his bathroom and went to the kitchen. Emma wasn't there and the fire was dying embers. The longer he had been with her, the more he had wanted her. Now he felt insatiable. Lovemaking should have cooled him. He had broken his own rules to avoid emotional and physical entanglements with employees. With Emma, he couldn't turn back time and now he didn't want to. Last night had been fantastic, red-hot and unforgettable, making him want her more than ever. He grew hot just thinking about her. She excited him beyond measure and was unbearably sexy. He hoped she didn't expect more than he could give because she was sentimental, someone he never expected to become involved with.

She was totally the type of woman he had always avoided going out with. Always, until now. They were captives of circumstances that placed them in the same room, close proximity day and night. There were too many sparks between them to avoid fire. When had he been unable to use more control or maintain his cool resistance and good judgment?

"Here I am," she said, coming through the door.

"You changed," he said, looking at her jeans and thick blue sweater. "You look great."

"I was just going to tell you that. And you also changed. I like your black sweater. And your tight jeans," she said, wriggling her hips.

"You'll never get dinner if you keep that up," he said, a husky note creeping into his voice as his temperature jumped just watching her twist her hips.

She held up a hand. "No, no. I get to eat."

"I know what I want."

"Let's try chili right now. If it isn't cooked beyond the point of being edible."

"Not at all. Cooker on low, remember? Rosie left us salads in the fridge. I'll get them before I serve the chili. Want a glass of wine or margarita first?"

She laughed. "I think we've done that before. We can't seem to get past it to dinner."

"It wasn't the drinks that interrupted. We'll try again. Do you want wine?"

"I'll take the margarita. Maybe this time, I'll actually drink one."

He left to mix her drink and she followed him to the bar.

"Before I forget," he said, "let me go get something that came in the mail earlier." He set down his bottle of beer and left to return with a large envelope. "Since you like family so much, here are pictures of our half sister's wedding to Garrett, our CFO and a longtime family friend. Bring your drink and we'll look at the pictures together."

She sat down on the sofa, and Zach sat beside her, removing a book of bound pictures from the envelope.

"Garrett has married Sophia, our half sister. We didn't know we had a half sister until the reading of Dad's will. You can imagine the shock, particularly to my mother. I thought we might have to call an ambulance and I'm not joking about it. She had no clue. No one could understand my dad. Not any of us, definitely not my mother. I don't think she even tried. Maybe Sophia's mother. He never married her, but he kept her in his life until the end."

"Sounds sad, Zach."

"Don't start feeling sorry for me over my dad. All of us wanted Sophia in the family. First, we really wanted her— that should please you. Second—Sophia, as well as all of us, stood to inherit a fortune from Dad if she became involved with the Delaney company. It was his way of forcing us to get her into the family. And forcing her to join us. Sophia was incredibly bitter over Dad and wanted no part of this family."

"Even though you were her half brothers?"

"That's where Garrett came in and you can see the results. We all like her and Garrett loves her."

Emma looked over the photographs. "She's beautiful and they both look radiantly happy."

"You're enough of a romantic to think that no matter what the picture shows."

Emma stuck her tongue out at him, making him grin.

He looked at her profile while she studied the pictures. Her skin was flawless, her lashes thick and had a slight curl. Locks of red hair spilled onto her shoulders. He set down his beer, took her drink from her hand and then placed it and the book of pictures on the table. He pulled her into his arms to kiss her.

Her mouth was soft, opening like the petals of a rose. Heat spilled in him, centering in his manhood. He couldn't get enough of her, relishing every luscious curve, her softness sending his temperature soaring. She wrapped her arms around him, kissing him in return, and he forgot dinner again.

Five

By Monday morning a bright sun made snow sparkle and icicles had a steady drip as ice and snow melted. When Emma went to the office she glanced out to see the snowman they had built Sunday afternoon. She had pictures of Zach clowning by the snowman.

Zach had run inside and returned with one of Rosie's aprons to put on the snowman. He removed the snowman's hat and placed sprigs of cedar for hair so he had a snow-woman. He posed for a picture with his arms around the snow-woman's waist and with Zach puckered to give the snow-woman a kiss.

Remembering, she smiled. They had turned the snow-woman back into a snowman because Zach said he needed to return Rosie's apron. She'd reminded him that *he* wore that very apron to cook their steaks Saturday nights, a point he'd conceded.

Monday was uneventful except she couldn't lose the constant awareness she had of Zach. She was getting too close to him, enjoying his company too much. The weekend had brought intimacy and an emotional bonding that she may have been the only one to experience. She thought about the job ending soon and not seeing Zach again, so the problem would resolve itself. In spite of the weekend, it seemed wiser to put the brakes on a relationship. How deeply did she want to get involved with him? They were totally different with different priorities and vastly different lifestyles. The weekend had been magical, but they were shut away into almost a dream world, isolated in the storm on the ranch. She should develop some resistance and keep from sinking deeper into growing close to him. At least she should try. The intimate weekend was over and she should avoid another if she could dredge up the willpower.

That evening she learned that he was having his dinner in the office. Disappointment was coupled with knowledge that she was better off not seeing him. As she filled her plate in the kitchen, she quizzed Rosie about how Zach spent his holidays and received the same version she'd heard from Zach.

"Christmas decorations are in the attic and haven't been touched in years because it's been so long since any of the family has been at the ranch at Christmas," Rosie said. "Nigel used to put them up in case the family came, but he stopped years ago because the Delaneys were rarely at the ranch in December. Actually, this house has been closed most of the time for the past ten years and the foreman runs the ranch."

Emma picked at her dinner, her focus on Rosie.

Peeling and cutting carrots, Rosie stood at the counter. "When Adam, Zach's eldest brother, was born, Mrs. Delaney was delighted and gave him her attention. He had a nanny and Nigel and I worked for them in the Dallas home. Back then, they had lots of help. By the time Will was born, Mrs. Delaney was losing interest. When Zach came along she wasn't happy and she told me herself—no more babies. They had their family."

"Rosie, that's awful," Emma said, thinking how every baby was so welcome in her family. Each birth was a huge celebration.

"That's the way she was. In those days she and Mr. Delaney were going their separate ways. When she got pregnant with Ryan, Mrs. Delaney had a screaming fit. She didn't want another child and she made that clear. She had lost interest in her boys."

"I can't imagine," Emma said, deep in thought about Zach.

"No. They were good boys. Adam was eight, Will was seven, Zach, five. She couldn't wait to get them out of the house and into boarding school. She sent Adam that year. Next year, Will went. Two years later, Zach went."

"That seems too young to send them away."

"Zach was never the same. He closed up and shut himself off. As a little fellow, he would hug me and climb into my lap. That all stopped. He was getting too big to get on my lap, but the hugs vanished. He was quieter, more remote."

"You and Nigel both seem to have a close relationship with him."

"Zach is nice to work for and I love him like another son, but he keeps his thoughts to himself. Any woman who thinks she'll come into his life and change him is in for a big disappointment."

"I can't imagine his solitary life," Emma said. "My family is like yours and we all gather together on holidays."

"Their mother just turned off the love, if she had ever really loved them. It hurt those boys. Maybe not Adam and Will so much because they were the oldest and had had more of her attention."

"I don't understand how she could do that."

"She's hardly ever laid eyes on Caroline who is her only

oldest grandchild, the daughter of Adam, who sadly passed
away. She has no interest in the little girl. Caroline is showered with love by all those around her, so I don't think she's
noticed or realized yet, but when she gets older, she will.
Mrs. Delaney's interest is in herself. She doesn't come see
them. Anyway, this is the first Christmas for a Delaney to
be here on the ranch in years. I don't think Zach pays much
attention to Christmas. He hasn't been home in years for a
holiday celebration."

"I can't imagine that either. At Christmas, home is the
only place I want to be."

"I agree," Rosie said, smiling broadly. "Open the pantry
door."

Emma did and saw snapshots of children, babies, adults,
teens.

"That's my family," Rosie said. "Zach has given me time
off and I will be with my family for Christmas." She wiped
her hands and came close to tell Emma the name and relationship of each person.

"That's wonderful, Rosie. I know you can't wait to see
them."

"Most are in Fort Worth, but others are scattered across
Texas. Dallas, San Antonio, Fredericksburg. I'll be off for
three weeks."

"This will be a fun Christmas for you," Emma said, wondering if Zach would enjoy being alone as much as he said
he did.

Later, while as she ran on the treadmill, Emma thought
about all Rosie had said. Emma suspected Zach would not
put up any Christmas decorations. She glanced at the ceiling, thinking about the room upstairs that led into the attic.
Emma's jaw firmed. She would decorate for Zach. She wanted
Christmas reminders in her room and on her desk, but while

she was at it, she would decorate the house a little if she found the Christmas decorations.

Nigel was gone by six each evening. By now Rosie might have left. As soon as she finished on the treadmill and showered, Emma pulled on fresh jeans and a red T-shirt. In the attic it took only minutes to find containers, systematically marked Christmas and each box had an attached list of contents.

She carried a box to the office and placed decorations around her area. She glanced toward Zach's desk and debated, leaving it alone except for one small Christmas tree she placed to one side.

Wondering whether she would encounter Zach, she carried another box to the family room. In the attic she had spotted a beautiful white Christmas tree covered in transparent plastic and tomorrow she intended to ask Nigel to help her get it into the family room.

Maybe the decorations would get Zach into the holiday spirit.

In the family room she placed artificial greenery on the mantel and then placed sparkling balls, artificial frosted fruit. She set long red candles in a silver candelabra in the dining room, arranging them on the mantel. The scrape of a shoe made her turn toward the door as Zach entered.

He stopped to glance around. His black T-shirt and faded, tight jeans set her insides fluttering.

"What are you doing?" he asked.

"Decorating a bit for Christmas since the holiday approaches."

Zach's gaze met hers as he crossed the room. "I don't care about your room or your desk. Otherwise, don't put this stuff up in the house. Your intentions are nice, but this isn't what I hired you to do," he said, stopping only a few feet away.

"I'm not using work hours to do this," she said. "I thought you'd like it."

"No. I don't want the clutter. It's old stuff and doesn't conjure up warm memories. I'll get Nigel to see that it's cleared away."

"I can take it out," she said. "I didn't know it would be hurtful."

"It isn't hurtful," he said, with a slight harshness to his tone. "I just don't want it around and it's time-consuming to put up and take down. Besides, you shouldn't be lugging those heavy boxes out of the attic. The decorations are meaningless. These are old decorations that should be tossed."

"You don't think your family, Caroline in particular, might enjoy them?"

His eyes narrowed. "I'm having an argument over Christmas decorations. Caroline's house in Dallas and the house in Colorado will probably be decorated from top to bottom. She doesn't need more here."

"You don't think she'll see you as Scrooge?"

"No, she won't. I'll have presents for her and she's so excited over the baby, she won't care what's happening here. Caroline has reverted back to a very happy child, which is what she was before she lost her dad. These decorations won't matter to her. When she's older, she'll accept me the way I am. Maybe view me as her eccentric uncle."

"Very well," Emma said quietly.

"I'm fine about Christmas and the holiday isn't about decorations. Stop looking at me as if I've lost my fortune or some other disaster has befallen me."

"I don't think losing your fortune would be as disastrous as what you are losing. And I know Christmas isn't about decorations. You childhood doesn't have to carry over in the same way now."

"Stop worrying about me being alone," he said, smiling,

his voice growing lighter as he stepped closer and placed his hands on her shoulders. His blue eyes were as riveting as ever. Her heart thudded and longing for his kisses taunted her.

He glanced around and walked to the big box of decorations to rummage in it.

"What are you doing?"

"What you wanted. I'll observe one old Christmas custom. There are some decorations I want."

Smiling, wondering what he searched for, she stepped closer.

"Here's one," he said, pulling out a decorative hanging cage filled with sprigs of artificial mistletoe. "I'll put mistletoe up all over this part of the house. Let's see if we can follow one Christmas tradition," he added, his tone lowering another notch, strumming over her nerves. "You can help with this."

"I don't think that's such a great idea," she whispered.

"I think it's fantastic." He attached the ornament to the hook on the top of the door, then stood beneath it. "You want some Christmas traditions in my life. Well, here's one," he said, winding his arm around her waist to draw her closer as he leaned forward.

His mouth was warm, his lips firm on hers. She opened to him, melting against him while her unspoken protests crashed and burned.

Wrapping her arm around his narrow waist, she held him tightly. Her heart thudded and she could feel his heart pounding. Desire fanned heat as an inner storm built.

Her moan sounded distant. Longing strummed over every nerve. She had intended to avoid moments like this, stay coolly removed from anything personal with him. Instead, she was tumbling into fires that consumed her. Need became a throbbing ache, more demanding than before.

Their passionate kiss lengthened, became urgent. She wound her fingers in the tight curls at the back of his neck.

Time vanished and the world around them disappeared. Zach's kisses were all she wanted.

How could it seem so right to be in his arms? To kiss him? They were far too different in every way that counted for it to seem like the best place to be when he held her. His kisses had become essential to her, yet their lifestyles clashed. She held him tightly as if his kisses were as necessary to her as the air in the room.

One hand wound in her hair while he kissed her, his other hand caressing her nape.

Finally, she leaned away. "Zach, this isn't what I planned."

He raised his head, his blue eyes filled with hunger. He glanced overhead. "I'm surprised the mistletoe hasn't burst into flames. Now I'm glad you got out the Christmas box. Let me see if there's more mistletoe in there." His husky voice conveyed lust as much as the flames in his crystal eyes. He turned to rummage in the box again. "Here are three more bunches. I have just the places. Come help me hang these."

"I still don't think I should. Zach, we're sinking deeper into something we were going to avoid."

"You started this. You can't back out now. C'mon." He left the family room and headed for the office, stopping in the doorway to hand her two of the bunches. "This is perfect," he said, giving her a long look that shivered through her. "You wait while I get a hammer."

He disappeared into the hall. Common sense urged restraint. Now she wished she had left Christmas decorations alone. In minutes he was back. She watched him reach up to push a tack into the wood to hold a sprig of mistletoe tied with a red ribbon. He tapped it lightly with the hammer. She passed him, crossing the office to her desk. She wanted space between them.

She could hear him hanging the mistletoe, but she didn't want to watch. She straightened her desk and wondered if she could tell him to take the last sprig and go. She would put the box of decorations away when Zach wasn't around. She had never thought about mistletoe, never expected to even see him tonight.

She thought about the sharp tone in his voice when he had first spotted the Christmas decorations. Was he all bottled up over old hurts? When it came to interacting with other people, from what she had seen, Zach was warm and friendly. Were old hurts still keeping part of him locked away from sharing life with those closest to him?

After he hung the mistletoe, he turned to her as he stood beneath it. "Emma, come here a minute."

"Don't be ridiculous," she said, wanting to laugh, yet feeling her insides clinch over his invitation.

"Emma, come here," he coaxed in a velvet tone.

"Zach," she said, sauntering toward him while thinking about his past, "I'll come there if you'll go somewhere with me either this week or next."

"Deal," he said, clearly not giving that much thought.

With her pulse racing, she stopped inches away from him.

He took her wrist to draw her to him. "Now we'll test this one," he said, framing her face with his hands as he placed his mouth on hers to kiss her again.

He tasted of mint while his aftershave held that hint of woods. She slipped her arms around his waist and kissed him. His arm banded her, pulling her close against him while he leaned over her and his kiss deepened.

When they paused, she took deep breaths, trying to get back to normal.

"We have a deal," she said. "Come home with me for the weekend and see what it's like to be with a family who wants to be together." She wanted him to see what a joy a loving family could be. Billionaire or not, she felt incredibly sorry for Zach, certain he was missing the best part of life and maybe with her family, he would see it. "When you see what you're missing, you'll want to start accepting your brothers' invitations to join them." Her last words tumbled out and she expected that curt tone and coolness he'd had earlier.

"You took advantage of me."

"Oh, please," she said in exasperation.

"Besides, I'm supposed to stay home to stay off my foot," he said. "I shouldn't be going anywhere for the weekend. That's the whole point of being stuck on the ranch." His voice held the husky rasp. His breathing was still ragged and his lips were red. His expression conveyed a blatant need that he made no effort to hide. Even though he argued, she suspected he was giving little thought to their deal.

"I'll drive and you can put your foot up in the car. At my folks' house, you can keep your foot elevated all the time you're there. We'll all wait on you. You'll have a good time."

"Emma, I don't want to go to my brothers' homes for holidays. Why would I go to your parents' when I don't know anyone except you?" he asked.

"Because you just agreed to do so."

He stared at her and she could feel a clash of wills and imagine the debate raging in his mind. "If I go home with you, won't your whole family think there's something serious between you and me?"

She smiled at him. "No. We all bring friends home a lot. Growing up, I'd say we often had at least one person eating with us who wasn't a family member."

"So how many men have you brought home?"

"None until now," she admitted. "It still doesn't mean anything other than you're my boss and I would like you to meet my family."

"Who takes her boss home to meet the family?" he asked and she was sure she blushed with embarrassment, but she wasn't giving up. Zach needed to see some real family life.

"As long as you're coming this weekend, you might as well come for Thanksgiving."

"Oh, hell, Emma, that's an extra two days."

"You said you would and you'll enjoy yourself and you can sit off in a room alone whenever you want and prop your foot up all you want."

"Dammit." He stared at her again with his jaw clamped shut and she was certain he would refuse. She felt silly for trying to get him to come. Her world-traveler billionaire boss was light-years away from her ordinary family.

"All right. If I'm going home with you for Thanksgiving, I get more than that one kiss," he said, pulling her back into his embrace and kissing her hard while he pulled her up against him. "A lot more," he added.

Startled, she was frozen with surprise for a few seconds and then her arms wrapped around his neck and she kissed him in return. His hand slipped down her back over her bottom, a long, slow caress, scalding even through the thick denim of her jeans.

His fingers traveled up again, slipping beneath her shirt, cupping her breast lightly, a faint touch causing streaks of pleasure. He pushed away the lacy bra, his warm fingers on her bare skin.

She moaned in delight, spreading her fingers wide and slipping her hand beneath his T-shirt to stroke his smooth, muscled back. Pleasure and need escalated swiftly.

Taking his wrist to hold his hand, she looked up. "Zach, we have to stop this for now. I can't—"

"Yes, you can" he said, showering kisses on her temple, her cheek, her throat. Protests faded into oblivion. She kissed and caressed him until he carried her to a bedroom where they made love for the next hour.

During the night she eased off the bed and slipped away from him, gathering her clothes as she went. She returned to her room, thankful for the space and the haven where she could be alone to think. In her own room, she fell into bed, her mind on Zach. Their lovemaking was binding her heart to him with chains that would hurt to break. Zach was becoming more important, more appealing and exciting. Was she tumbling headfirst, falling in love with him? A love that would never be returned. This past weekend, Zach had just become a bigger danger to her well-being and her heart. A weekend of love, three nights of passion, now another night. How long would it take her to get over what she already felt for him?

She fell asleep to dream about Zach and awoke early the next morning. Longing to go find him, kiss him awake and love again was strong. She slipped out of bed and looked at the clock, knowing she would follow a sensible course and get ready for a workday.

They both needed to step back and get things under control again. Just thinking about Zach, she wanted to be in his arms. Surprise lingered that she had asked him to go home with her and that he had accepted.

What had seemed a good idea at first, began to look like complication after complication. She had to let her family know. She thought about the family letters she had read and how little Zach cared and decided to hold him to his acceptance. She wanted him to see a family who relished being together and made the most of their moments. Maybe he would join his brothers more on holidays and participate with his own family.

Touching her lips lightly with her fingertips, she remembered his kisses. After Christmas she would return to her job in Dallas, and Zach would disappear from her life. She would be with him less than a month more. Despite her earlier worry, she *could* keep from falling in love with him because they had nothing between them except physical attraction. She didn't like his lifestyle, his attitude toward family, his disregard for all the things she loved so much. Maybe her heart was safe in spite of the attraction that was pure lust. She pulled out her phone to text her mother that company was coming. Company with an injured foot.

By Thanksgiving afternoon Zach wondered how he had gotten himself into this. Since he was twelve years old, he had been able to say no or get out of most things he didn't want to do unless it involved his father. Even with his father, by age twenty-one, he had become adept at escaping his father's plans for him.

He was in the center of a whirlwind. He had met four generations of Hillmans. They encompassed ages two to ninety-something. Brody, Emma's father, had made him feel welcome, as well as her mother, Camilla.

Zach tried to keep the names straight, learning her parents and siblings quickly. Connor, the married older brother, his wife, Lynne, Sierra, Emma's oldest sister, and Mary Kate, the youngest, both sisters married, Bobby, the younger brother. Zach mentally ran over the names of people seated around him while they ate the Thanksgiving turkey. He received curious glances from Connor and could feel Connor being the protective big brother even though they were far across the long table from each other.

The dining room table seated eighteen and other tables held more of the family with grandparents, aunts, uncles, nieces and nephews gathering together today.

Until the subject came up during the Thanksgiving feast, Emma had neglected to warn him that it was family tradition to decorate for Christmas after Thanksgiving dinner, which was eaten early in the afternoon. After dinner everybody under eighty years of age changed to jeans and T-shirts or sweatshirts. Also, the decorations didn't come out until the men had set up the Christmas trees in various rooms in the house, which they did while others cleared the tables.

Once trees and lights were up with an angel or a star at the top of each tree, the women and children took over with the decorations while the men decorated the porch.

As soon as Zach started to join the men, Emma took his arm to lightly tug him toward the living room. "You sit and elevate your foot. You can help the kids with the decorations. The little kids can't put the hooks on the balls and that sort of thing."

"Emma, I can do a few things outside."

"We need you in here and you know you should stay off your foot. The more you don't walk on it, the sooner you'll heal," she lectured, looking up at him with wide green eyes. His gaze lowered to her mouth and he longed to be alone with her and saw absolutely no hope until they left Dallas.

In minutes he began to help the little kids with ornaments while he sat with his foot resting on a footstool. Boxes of shiny trimmings were spread around him and on the table in front of him. Emma and her mother had a table over his propped-up foot to keep the kids from bumping his injury. The living room held what Emma had called the real Christmas tree. It was a huge live balsam pine that touched the ceiling. Spread around him were boxes of a family history of decorations with shiny ornaments mixed with clay and paper trimmings made by kids. Once Emma stopped beside him. "How are you doing?"

"You owe me," he said. "I intend to collect."

Her cheeks turned pink and he wondered what she was thinking. He remembered their lovemaking and wished with all his being he could be back at his ranch and alone with her. Instead, what seemed like a hundred people and kids were buzzing around him like busy bees. He had to admit she had a fun family and he'd had a good time through dinner. What he knew he would remember most, was when she had come down for Thanksgiving dinner. The whole family dressed for the occasion, which she had warned him about just before they had left the ranch.

He had been standing in the front hall and looked up as she came down the stairs. She wore an emerald green dress that came only to her knees and her red hair was caught up in a clip with locks falling free in the back. She looked stunning. The sight of her had taken his breath and he longed to be able to hold her and kiss her.

After a time Emma took away the table that sheltered his injured foot. "You're excused now to go watch football. They've finished decorating the porch and the guys turned on a game. We'll help the kids decorate and then clean up the Christmas tree mess. I'll take over your job."

"I don't mind doing this."

"Go watch football with the guys in the family room."

"You won't have to tell me again," he said, smiling at her and still wanting to kiss her. He stood and she slipped into his chair while he limped away.

During the second half of the game, his cell rang and he excused himself to answer Will's call.

"Happy Thanksgiving, Zach."

"Happy Thanksgiving to you and Ava and Caroline. Let me talk to Caroline," Zach said as he stepped farther into the hall so his conversation wouldn't interfere with everyone listening and watching football. He talked briefly to his niece and then Will came back on the line.

A touchdown was scored and the family members watching the game cheered and applauded.

"Where are you?" Will asked. "You sound as if you're at a game."

"I'm at Emma's house in Dallas," Zach admitted, certain there was too much background noise for him to convince

Will he was home alone at the ranch. He braced for what he knew was coming.

"You're where?" Will asked.

"You heard me. I sort of got finagled into this," he tried to say quietly.

"I can't hear you. You're at your secretary's house with her family?"

"That's right, Will. And I need to go. Happy Thanksgiving to you." As he ended the call, he was certain he had not heard the last from Will. Returning to his seat, he looked at the room filled with Hillman men and the older boys. This room held a huge white Christmas tree. Their attic had been filled to the brim with all the decorations that now covered the various trees in the house. With a deep sigh he settled to watch the game. The evening promised to be incredibly long, but he had to admit, the Hillmans had fun and obviously loved being together. To his surprise, he'd had a good time with them. They were nice people and her brothers were great to be around, actually making him miss seeing his own, which gave him a shock when he realized he was thinking about calling both of them, even though he'd just spoken to Will. He had to admit, Emma had been right about the weekend with her family versus his staying at the ranch by himself. He looked at her laughing at something her sister said to her. His insides knotted and he wanted badly to be alone with her and to hold her in his arms.

It took several hours to get the decorations up and the empty boxes put away. A sweeper was run. Finally the entire bunch of people settled in the family room, sitting on the floor, chairs, sofas. When the football game ended, Emma's sister, Mary Kate, sat at the piano to play Christmas carols and they all joined in singing. Emma came to sit beside him and to his amazement, the kids found him interesting, so they

had squeezed onto the sofa beside Emma and him. Being
crowded together suited him because he could put his arm
around Emma's shoulders without it seeming a personal gesture. He had an arm around two of the little kids on the other
side of him, but he enjoyed having Emma pressed against him.

To his surprise, he remembered the old songs he hadn't
sung in years. Finally when they stopped singing, they began
to pull coats out of closets.

"We're going outside because Dad turns on the Christmas
lights, a tradition that means the Christmas season is offi-
cially kicking off at the Hillman house."

Zach laughed. "I don't know how I let you get me into
this."

"I know exactly how," she said, giving him a sultry look
and his smile disappeared.

"Emma—" Smiling, she walked away and he watched her
hips covered in tight jeans as she walked away from him to
get her jacket.

The entire family and dogs gathered on the front lawn and
waited for the light ceremony. In minutes the lights came on
and it was bright as noontime. Zach stood next to Emma and
applauded with the others when the lights sparked to life.
"Emma, I've fallen into *Christmas Vacation*. This is the Gris-
wold house," he said softly.

She laughed. "Except the lights all came on at the first try.
Dad loves Christmas. Actually, we all do. It's wonderful."

The family stayed up talking until one when they began to
say good-night. By the time Emma and her younger brother,
Bobby, turned in, they had to lock up and switch off lights.

She had an apartment nearby, but she had told him she
would stay at her parents' house. He hadn't known they
wouldn't sleep at her place until they were almost to Dallas.
A huge disappointment to him.

At her door, Zach placed his hand on the jamb to block

her way. He tugged on a lock of her hair to draw her closer and leaned forward to brush her lips with a light kiss. The instant his mouth touched her soft lips, his body reacted. He ached with wanting her. His arm tightened around her waist while he kissed her long and fervently. "I want you, Emma," he whispered.

The look in her eyes made his pulse pound. He inhaled deeply, fighting the urge to reach for her again. This wasn't the time or the place, so he told her good-night before going to the room given to him for his weekend visit.

He wanted to be alone with Emma now and couldn't wait to get back to the ranch, but the holiday had been a pleasant surprise.

By Saturday, the weather had warmed. The family sat at a long picnic table, made from five tables pushed together with Zach at one end, his foot propped on a wooden box. Emma's mother was to his right and Emma sat on his left. Her father was at the far end while various relatives lined both sides of the table. They sat in a sunny spot in a wooded park not far from Emma's parents' home.

It was easy to see where Emma got her looks. Her auburn-haired mother, Camilla, was a good-looking woman and appeared far younger than she had to be since she was the mother of Emma's older brother and older sisters. Brody Hillman, Emma's dad, had welcomed him, but Zach could feel the unspoken questions and saw the speculation in Brody's expression. Even more open about his curiosity was Emma's older brother, Connor. Connor studied Zach and Zach could feel disapproval simmering just beneath the surface. Connor had been friendly, but only in a perfunctory manner and Zach thought it was just a matter of time before Connor quizzed him about his relationship with Emma.

There had been enough curious looks from all of them to

remind him that Emma did not bring men home with her fo the weekend. He had wished a hundred times over that he had not accepted her invitation, He would have to last until tomorrow afternoon when they would leave for his ranch.

"Zach," Emma said, "my nieces are so impressed with you. I told them you are a world traveler. They want to know the scariest trip you've had or scariest place you've been."

He smiled at a row of little girls staring at him expectantly and told about waking up with a huge snake in his tent, but that was not as scary as swimming and discovering a shark approaching him. By the time he got to that part, the boys had gathered around to listen. The girls sat quietly, their eye opening wider, and he didn't want to scare them. "Those were scary moments. Then there was a time I was camped fa from a town. My things kept disappearing. I thought some one who worked for me was taking them until I discovered it was a very sly monkey. We found the stash and I got back my things, except my golf cap. I left that for him and hoped I'd see him wearing it, but I never did."

As the girls laughed, he glanced at Emma to see her smil ing while she watched her nieces.

He got out his phone. "I have pictures," he said, opening it and quickly finding his electronic scrapbook. He held ou the phone and Emma had to join the kids to look. She gasped maybe only slightly less than the little girls. She bent closer looking at a massive snake that was held by four men.

"Zach, is it alive?" she asked.

"Yes, but it had been fed, so it wasn't moving much and everyone was safe."

She glanced at Zach, and he suspected he had just dropped a notch in her estimation of his lifestyle. He suspected she liked homebody types who spent their weekends playing with the kids versus someone who traveled and encountered wild snakes and ran some big risks.

After lunch, they cleaned up and when everything was put away, a tag football game was planned with everyone participating.

"You can be scorekeeper, Zach. We always have two or three scorekeepers, so no one person has to keep up with all of us," Brody said. "There's a lot of give and take to score-keeping for one of our family games. Usually we end up with about as many different scores as scorekeepers, so don't take any of this too seriously. You'll see."

Zach agreed to the task, sitting on the sidelines with his foot resting on a cooler. Brody's sister, Beth, joined him as scorekeeper along with Brody's mom, Grandma Kate. Emma's maternal grandmother, Grandma Nan, was on the field to play; she looked too young to be a grandmother. The oldest of the nieces and nephews was only six, so everyone played around the kids. As three-year-old Willie grabbed the ball and tried to run with it while the family cheered, Zach joined in, laughing at the child clutching the football as if it were a lifeline.

Zach glanced at Emma on the playing field. She had leaves in her hair. She had shed the bulky sweatshirt and wore a bright pink T-shirt with her jeans. She was watching him, laughing with him over the kids, and desire stabbed him. That electrifying tension flared to life, as unwanted and un-expected as it had been the first time she had walked into his home. He wished they were alone. Someone stepped between them and the tension eased, but it did not vanish.

The kids provided constant laughs with their antics and he saw why she liked to come home for the weekend. They were all happy with each other, having great fun. He had known fun with his brothers, but life had been tense if both his parents were present unless they were entertaining a house filled with their friends. Even then, it had never held this re-laxed closeness. He realized he was enjoying a whole family of people who loved each other and exhibited a joy in being together. He had this now with his brothers, but they seldom were all together and until Caroline, there had been no small children around.

He could see why Emma thought he was missing something and why she had hated to leave him alone. He looked at her parents, thinking how different they were from his own. The love they shared showed constantly even though they were across the field from each other, or at opposite ends of the long table earlier. He realized he had never seen that kind of warmth between his parents. He looked at Emma, laughing with a small niece. Maybe Emma was the wealthy one after all.

Breaking into his thoughts, he looked down into big brown eyes as a little boy walked up to him. "Did you give my team a point?"

He wasn't certain which child stood before him, guessing it was Jake. "Yes, I did give your team a very big point," he answered, amused that the little kid was checking on him.

The child nodded. "Thank you." He turned to his great-grandmother. "Did you give my team a point, Gran-Gran?"

"Yes, I did," she said, leaning forward to hug him. "You're playing a good game," she said.

"Thank you." Smiling broadly, he ran off, half skipped to his dad, who asked him a question, glancing over his head at Zach. The child told his dad something and his dad smiled at Zach and turned back to play.

Zach was unaccustomed to sitting out anything active. During the time-out, he motioned Emma over.

"I hate sitting on the sidelines. If three-year-old Willie can play, so can I."

"Zach, you have to stay off your foot."

"This shoe protects my foot. I am not accustomed to being a spectator. I'll stop if my foot hurts. It's only tag football."

"You'll be on my team then, so I can keep up with you."

"Don't hover. Your family will really think we have something going."

Zach got into the game, enjoying himself even though he knew he was being foolish and risking more injury, but he hated doing nothing except keeping score. He had never been one to sit on the sidelines and he didn't want to miss out now. He hobbled around and it was easy to keep up when they had geared down to a three-year-old level.

Before dinner they gathered wood to build a fire in a stone fireplace. When Zach started to help, Emma stopped him.

"This isn't a chore you have to do. Go sit and we'll get the wood."

"I'm not doing much," he said, brushing past her. Minutes later as he picked up a dead branch and turned, Connor blocked his way.

"Thought you were supposed to stay off your foot."

"A few branches and I'll quit. I still can't get accustomed to sitting around."

"Which is why Emma works on your ranch?"

"Right," Zach said. He could feel anger from Connor and see curiosity in his expression.

"You've been all over the world, so you're pretty sophisticated and experienced. Emma's not. Did she tell you she's never brought anyone home before?"

"We work together. I don't know what she's told the family, but I think I'm here because she feels sorry for me."

"Yeah. We heard you were alone. I just don't want to see my sister hurt."

"I wouldn't want her hurt either."

"Zach," Emma called, hurrying to join them. "Give those sticks to Connor and come sit. You shouldn't be on your foot. Just watch everyone."

All the time she talked, Zach looked at Connor who gazed

at him with a flat stare that held a silent warning. When Emma tugged on his arm to take the wood from him, Zach turned away.

"I think Connor was being a big brother and jumping to ridiculous ideas. Pay no attention to him," she said.

"Your older brother is a little difficult to ignore since he's five inches over six feet tall and probably weighs in at 250."

"Come on. They're getting the fire started and we'll cook dinner and then sit and sing and later, tell stories."

Amused, he went with her, hobbling along.

As they got dinner on the tables, Emma carried a hot dish and set it on the table, then turned to find Connor beside her.

"Emma." He glanced over her head and she realized they were the only two standing at the end of the long table. "Be careful. I don't want you to get hurt."

"I hope, Connor, you didn't threaten him. He's my boss."

"If that's all he is, that's fine. Guys like Zach Delaney do not marry into families like the Hillmans."

"I brought him home for the weekend because I didn't want him to spend Thanksgiving alone. We've always invited people who might be alone on holidays. I felt sorry for him. There's nothing more to it than that."

"It looks like more," Connor said, frowning.

"This is a temporary job that is on the verge of ending. When it does end, I'll never see him again. Most of the time he works abroad. There's nothing to be concerned about."

"I hope not. Take care of yourself."

She smiled. "I will. Stop worrying."

He jammed his hands into his pockets and walked away. She watched him and shook her head. Connor was forever the big brother.

As she got more dishes of food on the table, Mary Kate approached with more delicious looking food.

"Is Connor being big brother?" she asked.

"Ever so," Emma replied, rolling her eyes.

"Emma, *should* Connor be big brother?"

"No. I didn't want Zach to be alone over the holiday and e would have been. Anyone in this family would have inited him if they had been in my place."

"Are you sure?" Mary Kate asked, tilting her head to study er sister. "Here he comes." She moved away before Emma nswered. She forgot her siblings. Zach approached and he vas the only person she noticed.

After dinner they played a word game around a blazing ampfire. When the sun went down the air cooled with a fall hill and the fire felt good. Emma sat close beside him and ach longed to put his arm around her, but he did not give in o the impulse. It would look far too personal for a boss and ecretary. The dancing red flames highlighted gold streaks in mma's hair. She sat beside him playing a simple game where ey sang and clapped and the little kids could play. Emma's ad sat with his arm around her mother while she clapped.

Zach continued to marvel at her family. Outside of old ovies, he hadn't known families like this really existed. He ompletely understood why Emma treasured her weekends at ome and her holidays. As a little kid he had hoped for this, ut it had never happened with his own family or any that he isited and he finally had come to the conclusion such famies did not exist, but Emma was proving him wrong.

Once as she sang, she glanced at him and smiled. More an ever, he wanted his arm around her or just to touch her, ut he knew that wasn't a possibility now. If he wasn't care-l, her family would have them engaged.

It was after ten when they began to break up. He helped ean until he was told to put his foot up. Finally he went with mma back to her parents' house. Tonight, everyone was eading home except her younger brother, and Zach wanted return to her apartment and be alone with her.

Instead, they sat up talking to Bobby until one in the morning. While Bobby and Emma talked about Bobby's school year, Zach looked at the Christmas tree. He had counted eight Christmas trees of various types and sizes that had been set up and decorated in the Hillman home.

Besides celebrating Thanksgiving, he was immersed in Christmas. The mantels in the family room and living room were covered in greenery and red bows. Decorations were everywhere he looked. No wonder she had tried to decorate the ranch a little. His attention shifted to Emma and his longing to be alone with her increased.

Finally, when Bobby went to bed half an hour later, Emma came to sit by him. He made room for her and she leaned against his chest, his arm around her and her feet beside his on the sofa.

"It's been fun, Emma. You have a great family."

"You really mean that?" she asked, twisting to look at him. She was in his arms, her face so close to his. "I love Thanksgiving," she said, turning and settling back against him. "I love Christmas. Look at the tree. It's beautiful and so many ornaments remind me of a special thing or person or time. I couldn't bear Christmas without a tree."

"I'm not as tied in to Christmas as you well know by now."

"You should get into the spirit and enjoy Christmas. I you did, you would never return to spending it the way you do now." She yawned and stretched. "I'm ready to turn in Zach." She stood and he came to his feet. She walked to the tree and carefully lifted free a glass Santa to show to him "This is my favorite."

He looked at the ornament and her delicate, warm hand "I hope you have years of wonderful Christmases," he said quietly.

"I hope you do, too."

"This is turning into one so far."

"It's Thanksgiving and the start of the Christmas holiday. There's a month to go." She returned the Santa to the tree. "I love each ornament, Zach." He came to stand beside her and put his arm around her waist. "Look at our reflection," she said, touching a shiny green ball.

"I'm going to start carrying a sprig of mistletoe in my pocket," he said, turning her to him to kiss her.

His arm tightened around her waist and she slipped her arms around him, kissing him while her pulse drummed. She quivered while desire ignited. Finally, she raised her head. "We should go to bed."

"If only you would always say that at the ranch," he replied. He smiled and kept his arm around her waist to walk beside her as they headed toward the stairs.

"Night, Zach," she said and disappeared into the room where she slept. In his own room, he lay in bed with his hands behind his head, thinking about the day and the evening with her and her family. He couldn't imagine spending every weekend this way, but sometimes it would be fun. He still thought she was missing out on a wonderful world and when his foot was healed, he would try to show her some place exciting out of Texas since she had never even been beyond the boundaries of the Lone Star state. As soon as he thought of traveling with her, he knew it would never happen. When the job ended, she would go out of his life. She had been correct when she said they had vastly different lifestyles. Neither one was the right person for the other in even a casual way.

In spite of that knowledge, his common sense, caution and experience, he couldn't stop wanting her and he couldn't shake her out of his thoughts.

He finally drifted to sleep, still yearning to be alone with her.

After Sunday dinner, Zach and Emma left for the ranch. She drove again while he sat with his foot propped up across the backseat and resting on bags placed on the car floor.

"You have a nice family. I see why you value your weekends. Your family shows they enjoy being together."

"Thank you. You seemed to like being with your brother and his family."

"I do, but I don't think my brothers and I have the closeness your family does."

Emma could see Zach in the rearview mirror. "You can have that closeness. From what you've said, you're all congenial. Maybe you are alone so much because you keep up your guard, Zach. It might carry over from childhood and times you were alone. Life's different now. You don't have to keep everything all bottled up. You can enjoy your brothers and now there's a half sister. You and Will seem very close."

He sat in silence. She met his gaze when she glanced at him, but then she had to turn her attention back to the road. "You might be right," he said finally. "I've never looked at it that way. I was disappointed as a kid. So were they. We were dumped and couldn't even be home together some years. I don't know—maybe my feelings are a guard left from childhood hurts. As a little kid, I couldn't keep from resenting it."

"Well, the nice thing now is that you don't have to be alone," she said, smiling at him.

"Maybe you're right. I'll admit it's fun when my brothers are together. And now I enjoy having Caroline and Ava there, too. Your family certainly has a great time together."

"We do and in a crunch, we can count on each other too. I'm happy you came with me."

"I enjoyed the weekend. Neither of your brothers were thrilled. I got looks from them the whole time. If they intended to send me warnings, they succeeded."

"Pay no attention to them. You'll never see them again."

Zach smiled and looked at her as she glanced in the rear-view mirror at him. "I'm not invited back?"

Emma felt her cheeks flush. "Of course you are. When-ever you would like to go home with me. I just figured you wouldn't want to again. I sort of trapped you into this time."

He grinned. "I'm teasing you."

"Zach, would you like to come home with me for Christmas?" she asked sweetly. "We'll have the whole family and they would be delighted to have you."

"No, they wouldn't be delighted. Thank you for asking me. I'll stay home and give my foot a rest."

"They would be pleased to see you again, except perhaps Connor, but you can ignore him."

"Home on the ranch is where I belong."

When they stepped inside the empty ranch house, Zach dropped their bags and switched off alarms. As she picked up her bag, he turned to take it from her and set it back on the floor. He slipped his arm around her waist. "Now what I've waited all weekend to do," he said in a husky voice. "You do owe me."

Six

When his mouth covered hers, her heart lurched. Wrapping both arms around his neck, she pressed tightly against him. His mouth was warm, insistent, and she kissed him eagerly. She clung to him, returning his kiss while the air heated and her heartbeat thundered. How could he melt her in seconds? Why did he weave such a spell with her? She didn't care. All she wanted at the moment was to hold and kiss him. She felt as starved to make love as they had on the snowy weekend.

"Emma, I want you," he whispered.

Each kiss was more volatile than the last. At the moment she didn't care about caution and what was wise in dealing with him. All she wanted was to be in his arms and kissing him.

Still kissing her, he picked her up and carried her through the house to the family room. He sat on the sofa, cradling her on his lap. Her hands drifted over him while her heart raced. She was glad they were together. Running his fingers in her hair, he kissed her. Why did this seem necessary? Why did his loving seem so right and special? The questions were dim, vague speculation that was blown away by passion.

She combed her fingers through his thick curls and played her hand over his muscled chest.

His hand slipped beneath her T-shirt. His fingers were warm, his hand calloused and faintly abrasive against her skin, a sensual, rough texture that heightened feeling. In seconds he had pushed away her bra to caress her. Pleasure streaked from his slightest touch, fanning sexual hunger to a bigger flame. Emma sat up, her thick red hair falling on both sides of her face as she tugged his T-shirt free and pulled it over his head. His eyes darkened and he had her shirt whisked away in a flash.

Knowing she was pursuing a reckless course, but wanting him desperately, she sat astride him and leaned forward. They embraced each other to kiss, his sculpted, warm chest pressed against her with the mat of chest curls a tantalizing texture.

Desire raged while she struggled to dredge up control. Dimly, she thought about her fears of how hurt she would be when the job ended and she told Zach goodbye. The hard knowledge that when that time came, he would be gone permanently from her life was a cooling effect. And it hurt. Was she falling in love with him? Was she *already* in love?

She leaned away slightly to frame his face with her hands. "To my way of seeing, our continuing to make love is a road to disaster. I want to back up a little and think about what we're doing." As she talked, she shifted off Zach and stood in front of him. While he watched her, his fingers caressed her, dallying along her hip and down her thigh, causing her to pause. She inhaled sharply, closed her eyes and stood immobile while his hands created magic and made her want to go back to kisses and loving him.

After seconds or minutes, she didn't know, she grabbed his wrists and opened her eyes. "Zach, wait."

He stood, his arms wrapping around her. She ran her hands over his chest. "I want you, Emma. I want to make love to you all night."

"Part of me wants that. Part of me has enough sense to know that's a reckless course to follow. Getting involved with you isn't what I hired on to do. And that first day that's what you agreed to avoid. I don't want last weekend every night until this job is over. If we do, I'll never want to leave."

"I just know what we both want right now. Kisses don't have one thing to do with business or your job or mine. I wasn't even going to keep you that first day, but you proved to be such a damn good secretary, I did. Emma, I've spent the past four days wanting you. I've been with you, watching you, aching to hold and kiss you."

His words echoed her feelings. Constantly through the holiday, she had glanced at him, wanting to go somewhere they could be alone to kiss and love and lose themselves as they had the weekend before. At the same time, she knew the hopelessness of getting more deeply entangled with him.

"You and I are way too opposite to get closely involved. You might not care at all and that means nothing to you, but it means a lot to me. You saw my family. My lifestyle and background are totally different from yours. If we continue to make love now, it will mean certain things on an emotional level to me that lovemaking won't to you. We'll get more deeply involved with each other. I can't separate that from my deepest feelings."

Standing, he reached out to take her into his arms again. "We'll just kiss. You say when to stop."

"If we do this, Zach, you'll have my heart."

"Maybe you'll have mine," he whispered, showering kisses on her temple to her cheek and then on her mouth. He kissed her insistently, holding her close against him, ending her arguments. She wanted him and her hunger overcame the logic, her caution, her arguments. She held him, kissing him with fervor that grew. The weekend had been another chain binding her heart. She held him tightly. She couldn't stop now. Later, he picked her up, kissing her as he carried her to the closest bedroom to make love to her.

Near dawn she stirred and rolled over to look at Zach who lay sleeping beside her. She rose up, brushing a curl off his forehead. A dark stubble covered his jaw. He was muscled and fit except for his injury that would heal. With their loving and Zach going home with her, he became more appealing each day. It didn't matter. There was no way he could ever be the man for her. No matter what her heart wanted. They were far too opposite. Even if they both were wildly in love, there was no possibility she could ever accept his lifestyle. She had told him if they continued making love, it would mean more to her and it would hurt deeply when she had to break it off and leave. And should he want her to stay, or wanted to marry her, which was impossible with a man like Zach, she couldn't accept. Not with his nomadic lifestyle.

While he had been good about the weekend with her family, she suspected there was no likelihood he would ever settle. She hurt and the hurt would grow worse later, but they were mismatched and neither wanted change.

He had met her family now and knew enough about her that he should understand what she told him. She suspected this job would end soon because he had a doctor's appointment this week and she had noticed he was getting around far better each day.

She studied him, with his shadowy long lashes on his cheeks. As he slept, she took her time. Looking at his firm lips, she thought about their kisses. Unable to resist, she leaned closer to kiss him lightly. His arm banded her waist and his eyes opened lazily. He pulled her close to kiss her to make love. She stopped thinking and gave herself to feeling.

At nine o'clock, she sat up and reached across him to get his phone from a bedside table. "Zach, it's after nine. We have to—"

He kissed her and stopped her announcement. In minutes he raised his head. "We don't really have to do anything except stay here in bed."

"Oh, yes, we do," she said, stepping out of bed and tugging free the sheet to wrap around herself. "We need to get back to our business relationship. We're already deep enough in a personal one. It's time to slow this part down." He placed his hands behind his head, smiling and watching her.

"I'll see you in the office," she said, scurrying out of the room, praying she didn't encounter Nigel before she got away from Zach and got her clothes back on.

It was an hour before she had showered and dressed in fresh jeans, a blue cotton shirt and loafers. With an eagerness she couldn't curb, she went downstairs to the office to find Zach sitting behind his desk.

He smiled when she came in and stood to come around his desk. He looked sexy, more appealing than ever in fresh, tight jeans and a black sweater. The warmth in his eyes held her immobile, unable to look away, and her pulse drummed in her ear. Her breath caught as he closed the distance between them to take her into his arms and kiss her a long time.

"Good morning," he said in a deep voice that was like fur wrapping around her.

"Good morning," she whispered in return, aware she was in love with him to the extent she might not ever get over it. This was a man she absolutely had to get over. He would never be the man for her and she could never be the woman for him.

"We weren't going to do this in the office. Use some self-control," she teased, trying to make light of the moment and end it.

"Sure. For now," he replied, heading to his desk. As Zach circled his desk, she noticed that he no longer limped and she was certain he would be able to go back to his normal life very soon and would no longer need her. The thought of telling him goodbye hurt with a pain that ran deep. She had faced the truth that she was in love with him. Hurt was inevitable.

They both were busy and lunch was brief, but he ate with her and she was glad. She wanted to be with him and the clock was ticking. Their time together would end too soon. She wanted more than just dining with him, of course, but each time they made love, her heart was bound more tightly with his.

Zach sat with work in front of him, but he couldn't keep from continually watching Emma. She was filing, moving around from desk to file cabinet, paying no attention to him. The tight jeans molded her hips and long legs. Her hair was tied behind her head with a ribbon and through lunch he had wanted to reach over and untie it.

He should have told her goodbye when they got back last night and he should have eaten lunch on his own today. He thought about her brother; he had meant it when he had told Connor he didn't want to hurt Emma. He glanced at his desk calendar. He would go to the doctor tomorrow and he suspected he would be told he had recovered and could return to his usual activities, which meant her job would be over.

If someone had bet him everything he owned that he would go home with a secretary who was a homebody deluxe, he would have lost every cent he owned. All during the ride back in the car, he had longed to lean over the seat to kiss her. When they arrived home, their lovemaking was inevitable. He could not resist.

He thought of what she had said in the car about the way he was with his family. Was his solitary life because he didn't know how to open up with his brothers or risk his emotions again and get them trampled as he had when he was a child?

He was leaving the ranch and the country as soon as he could. He would probably spend Christmas in Italy. He thought about the fun she would have with her family and couldn't keep from comparing that with thoughts about him rattling around the house in Italy all alone. The Italian home didn't hold near the appeal it had a month earlier.

Thoughts of her heated him. He wanted her right now and he wanted her in his bed again tonight. What would it be like to marry Emma and have her in his bed each night? The question shocked him because it was the first time he had contemplated even a thought of marriage with any woman he was friends with. How emotionally entangled was he with Emma? She stirred responses and emotions in him no other woman ever had. But there was no way he could have a permanent relationship with her.

She made her choices and she knew the job would end soon and they would part and not see each other again. There was absolutely no future in seeing her after she returned to Dallas. This wasn't the woman for him. Except in bed. He couldn't get enough of her there. Just watching her and thinking about her, he was getting aroused.

Knowing he had to get his mind off her and cool down, he turned to pick up the weekend mail, trying to concentrate on business.

It was almost four when Zach's phone rang. Emma had closed her computer and it looked as if she were clearing her desk to get ready to go. Zach answered the phone to hear Will.

Zach turned to ice, swearing quietly, causing Emma to look at him. "I'll be there as fast as I can get there." He replaced the phone.

"Caroline's gone," he said, glancing at Emma as he punched a number on his cell phone while he came around his desk.

"Oh, no. How long ago?" Emma rushed to keep up with him. She hurried beside him. "What happened? What will you do?"

"Go look for her. You can stay or you can come with me." Zach broke off to talk to his foreman. "Carl, Zach. Caroline's dog ran off and she went after it. They don't know where she is. Organize the guys and get them to head over to Will's ranch to help look for her. I'm going now." He listened and then ended the call. He grabbed a jacket he kept in the back hallway. He tossed her one of his. "Take this if you're coming with me."

She yanked on the heavy jacket, half running to keep up with him.

"Will and Ava are in Dallas. They were going to the symphony," Zach explained as they hurried toward the eight-car garage. "They're flying back now."

"How did Caroline disappear?"

"Muffy got out and Caroline went after her. The nanny, Rosalyn, went after Caroline, but Rosalyn slipped and fell. They think she hit her head on a rock because she lost consciousness briefly. When she regained consciousness, Caroline was gone." He was tempted to tell Emma to stay at the ranch because he could go faster without her, but they probably would need everyone they could get to help search for Caroline. His insides were a knot thinking about the little girl wandering around on the ranch with night coming.

"Thank heavens the weather is warmer than last week," Emma said, half running to keep up with his long stride.

"Will already has a chopper in the air and he's calling Ryan. He'll notify the county sheriff after he talks to Ryan," Zach said. He was chilled with fear for Caroline and couldn't wait to get to Will's ranch to start searching. Hazards spun in his mind and he tried to not think about them. How long would it take Caroline to get to the highway? From what Will said, she must have been near the house when last seen. He'd think forty minutes to an hour at best before she could possibly reach the highway. He glanced at the sky. It probably would be dark in another two hours.

"Damn, there are some canyons and some woods on Will's land," he said. "She's just so little."

Climbing into a pickup, with Emma rushing into the passenger seat, Zach headed toward the highway pushing the truck as fast as he dared.

Emma called her mother, relaying the situation. "My family can at least say a few prayers," she explained to Zach. "How long has Caroline been gone?"

"Not long. The minute she regained consciousness, Rosalyn called Will on her cell, so it was just a brief time. The bad thing was Rosalyn had no idea which direction to go to look for Caroline."

"Surely she hasn't gone far from home. Maybe she'll find her way back soon."

"She'll be chasing that little dog," he said, explaining about how easily Caroline could find her way to the highway. "Little kids can go fast sometimes and they like to run."

"I think we'll find her. She hasn't had time to get far."

"We've got a creek that has a few deep spots. She swims, but it's cold and I don't know what she'd do if she panicked. We have rattlesnakes in abundance," he said, clamping his mouth closed. "At least it's winter and the snakes won't be the same problem as in summer," he said, aware he was thinking out loud. Caroline was too little, her life too sheltered, to have any idea how to take care of herself.

"Hope for the best, Zach," she said, looking every which

way out the windows. "I know she can't be this far out, but I can't keep from looking around."

He gritted his teeth. He couldn't understand Emma's hopeful tone as if finding Caroline had become a certainty. There had been only rare moments in his adult life he had felt terrified, but he did now. He never had to this extent.

The car left a cloud of dust in the graveled road as he sped along, sliding on curves, sending plumes of dust into the air. They reached the highway in record time and he was amazed his driving hadn't scared Emma. Feeling a grim foreboding, Zach pushed the truck to its limit, speeding on the flat road. He gripped the steering wheel until his knuckles hurt.

"When we get close to Will's land, especially in line with the house, should you slow to watch for her?"

"I'm going to the house to find out where Rosalyn last saw her. We have to find her before night falls. We have mountain lions, coyotes. She can't stay out alone tonight."

"She can't have gotten far," Emma said with a strong, positive tone. "We'll find her before dark. We'll split up to look," Emma said. "No point in staying together. Maybe Muffy will just go home."

"I don't think so," Zach replied, his nerves on edge and not helped by Emma's cheerful optimism. "That little dog isn't any more accustomed to being out on her own than Caroline is. Muffy won't know the way home. Damn, I've never felt so helpless."

"Have you ever been this panicked about yourself?"

He gave her a startled look. "That's entirely different."

"Have you ever been this concerned about another adult?"

"No. Adults are different. Caroline is vulnerable."

"You're going to help. There are lots of people to help in the search. I'm sure we'll find her."

"Emma, I don't know how you can be so certain we'll find her," he said, trying to avoid snapping at her. "All the odds are the other way." If he and Emma were opposites, it had never been more so than at this moment. He glanced at her and saw her watching the land spreading away from the county road.

"There are a lot of people to look for her and she hasn't been gone long," Emma replied.

She was right, but it was a huge ranch with too many hazards for a child. Caroline would be completely unpredictable because she had never been out alone before. He hurt for Will and Zach was terrified for Caroline, trying to avoid thinking about how afraid she must be.

They lapsed into another silence until Zach waved a hand. "We're less than a mile from the turn into Will's ranch."

A barb wire fence bounded the property and the land near the road was flat with mesquite scattered across it. "You can see a lot from here." Shortly, he spotted the gate ahead and beyond it a thick grove of trees. The road curved out of sight and two tall cottonwoods bordered the county road. "Let me out along here, Zach," Emma said.

"I don't think she's had time to get this far. I hope not."

"I'll start walking back toward the house. Maybe I'll meet her." She patted his arm. "Don't worry until you have to."

"How the hell can I not worry?" he snapped, knowing he was being sharp, but he was filled with worry and fear for Caroline and he couldn't understand or appreciate Emma's positive attitude.

"Let me out as soon as you turn off the highway please."

"Emma, I don't want to have to worry about you, too."

"Don't be ridiculous. I have my phone. Stop the car and I'll go on foot."

He slowed, turned and stopped.

"Be positive, Zach. We'll find her." She jumped out quickly and he drove away.

At least she had a phone and knew how to use it. He suspected Emma knew little more than Caroline about being out on her own on the ranch, but she was an adult and would be okay. She was insulated in her positive feelings while he had none. As he drove around a bend in the road, Emma disappeared from sight in his rearview mirror.

Emma stood still, her gaze searching the dark woods. It would be five soon and since it was winter, the daylight would fade quickly. Saying another prayer, she began to walk inside Will's fence, continuing on in the direction they had been headed before Zach turned onto the ranch drive. She had told him she would walk toward the house, but she wanted to look along the highway a bit first. The highway worried Zach and she could see why. She studied the darkness beneath the thick grove of trees as she went. Surely if a child and a dog were nearby, they would make noise.

"Caroline," Emma called, the cry sounding small, pointless in all the emptiness around her.

Emma walked briskly for ten minutes, following the wide curve of the road, listening for any sounds of a child and then she heard voices. The road still curved and whoever was talking was lost to sight, but it sounded like more than two people.

Emma jogged, following the road, and finally she saw a pickup ahead. It had pulled off the side of the road. Relief and joy swamped her because it was a couple standing and talking to Caroline. The child held a white dog in her arms.

"Caroline!" Emma lengthened her stride and ran, breathing deeply when she reached them.

"Caroline, everyone is looking for you," she said as she hugged the little girl lightly.

She looked expectantly at the couple standing watching. She offered her hand. "I'm Emma Hillman," she said.

"We're Pete and Hazel Tanner," a deeply tanned, white-haired man said. His wide-brimmed hat was pushed back on his head. "We saw the dog and stopped and in a few minutes the little girl came running into sight. She gave us a number to call and they are coming to get her."

"Thank you so much," Emma said. "I'll call her uncle and tell him in case he hasn't gone to the house." She turned slightly, calling Zach to tell him.

"I'm the one coming back to get her," Zach said. "When I drove up, they told me the Tanners had called. Thank goodness you're with them. I should be there in minutes."

"She's fine, Zach. And she has her dog with her. These nice people stopped to see about Muffy and then Caroline came along."

"Just wait and I'll get all of you. I won't be long."

"I'm sure you won't," she said smiling and thinking how fast he had driven. She called her mother to let her know Caroline was found safe.

Scratching Muffy's head while Caroline held her, she talked to the couple for a few minutes. She wanted a hand close to the dog in case Muffy decided to run again.

"Caroline told us her name and how her little dog ran away and she couldn't catch her. She said her nanny was probably looking for her," Mabel Tanner said.

"A lot of people are searching for Caroline," Emma stated, smiling at the girl.

Emma heard the car before she saw Zach and then she watched him pull onto the shoulder to park. He had a leash in his hand and hooked it on Muffy's collar after he had hugged Caroline. Picking up Caroline, he handed the end of the leash to Emma while he talked to the Tanners.

"Thanks beyond words for helping," he said, shaking hands with the couple and talking briefly to them. In minutes they climbed into their pickup while Zach held the door for Emma and Caroline. As Caroline buckled herself into the back, Zach buckled the leash in beside her. Caroline pulled Muffy onto her lap. Zach leaned in to brush a kiss on the top of Caroline's head. "You gave us a real scare," he said softly.

"I'm sorry." She smiled up at him, and he stepped back to close the door.

He slid behind the wheel and glanced at Emma. "After I talked to you and knew you were with Caroline, I called Will to tell him to go on to the symphony because everything is okay here. He's already landing. He said he wants to come home to hug Caroline."

"I can understand that," Emma answered. She turned in her seat to talk to Caroline.

"Caroline, did you have trouble finding Muffy?"

"No. I could see her, but she wouldn't come back to me. I had to run fast."

"I'll bet you did," Emma replied. "You ran a long, long way."

Caroline nodded her head. "She sat to wait for me and then she'd run. I think she wanted to play."

Emma had to laugh. "I'm sure she had great fun."

"Everyone was very worried about you and Muffy. I'm glad we found you and Muffy didn't cross the highway," Zach said.

"Mr. and Mrs. Tanner told me that they saw Muffy and stopped because they thought she was a lost dog. Then they saw me. When I told them I was alone, they called Daddy Two. I told them his phone number."

"That was the right thing to do," Zach said. "He'll be here soon."

Caroline's eyes narrowed. "Am I in trouble?"

"I don't think so," Zach said. "We'll just be glad to have you and Muffy home again. Rosalyn is very worried. We all were worried about where you were and if you were safe. You gave us all a big scare, Caroline," he said.

"I would have gone home, but I couldn't catch Muffy."

"Would you have known how to find home?" Zach asked her.

"I could have followed the fence. Except I got scared when I saw Muffy running toward the highway."

"I'll bet you were scared. How did Muffy get loose?"

"The back gate wasn't closed all the way. Someone had left it open and Muffy squeezed out."

"Well, we'll put a little sign on that gate to keep it closed," Zach said and Caroline smiled.

Caroline hugged Muffy who had stretched out to sleep. "Thank you for coming to get me, Uncle Zach."

"You're welcome," he said.

Soon they were home and as they approached the house, Rosalyn waited on the porch. Pulling her coat close around her, she came down the steps to greet them. With a bandage on her forehead, she looked pale and she walked slowly, carefully hanging to the rail.

"Rosalyn doesn't look so great," Zach said quietly.

They climbed out of the car, and Caroline ran to Rosalyn to hug her while Zach got Muffy out and held her until they were inside the fenced yard. He set the small dog on her feet to remove her leash.

Emma greeted Caroline's nanny and stood quietly while Zach talked to her about her fall. "You should get off your feet, Rosalyn."

"I will. I just had to come hug Caroline. She didn't know I fell. She thought I was probably coming behind her. I can't tell you how worried I've been. About as much as Mr. Will. I caught my foot on a root and I couldn't keep from falling. I hit something, and then I was just out. When I came to, Caroline was gone. I've never had such a scare," she said, looking at Caroline who was tossing a ball for Muffy.

"She's back with her dog so you mend. Take it easy and get well."

"I intend to," she said, smiling at him.

A car came up the drive and Will spilled out, hurrying around to open the door for Ava. They both rushed through the gate. The instant Caroline saw them, she threw out her arms and ran toward them.

Will picked her up to hug her and hold her out so she and Ava could hug.

"We'll go say hello and goodbye. Leave the family to themselves," Zach said.

Will turned to greet them, shaking Zack's hand. "Thanks for coming on the run and thanks, Emma, for finding her with the Tanners on the highway. They live over in the next county and we know each other to say hello. I couldn't believe Caroline made it to the highway in that time."

"We're all happy now," Zach said. "We'll leave you to talk to Caroline and Rosalyn. Night, sweetie," he added, kissing Caroline's cheek. Slipping a small, thin arm around his neck, she hugged him and Zach smiled at her.

He took Emma's arm to go to his car and in minutes they were on the road driving back to his ranch.

"I'm going home, kicking back and having a beer. Caroline looks so little and frail. That scared me. I still feel as if my insides are shivering." He glanced at her. "How did you keep so calm?"

"You were calm."

"I just had it all bottled up, but it's coming out now."

Emma was amazed, because Zach seemed so tough, and today, cool when he had taken charge to call his men and then get to Will's ranch quickly. He had traveled and worked in dangerous jobs all over the world where he'd had to keep his wits, yet now he was coming apart. She saw his hands had a tremor. "I don't know how you were calm," he repeated.

"Positive thinking and prayers, Zach. Expecting a happy outcome."

"You're the eternal optimist," he stated, shaking his head. "I've seen too much, Emma. Positive thinking and prayers can't guarantee happy endings."

"Neither can giving up hope and imagining all sorts of scary scenarios. Then if something happens, because of your imagination, you've suffered more than once. We're very different people."

"Amen to that one," he said. "There's the one thing we can agree about," he added and she smiled.

As soon as they were inside the house, Zach built a fire, got the wine she requested and a beer for himself. While he sipped, he stretched out on the floor. Firelight flickered over him and her breath caught. He looked virile, appealing. Broad shoulders, long legs, thick curls. She wanted to join him, but that was a path to deeper complications.

"How do people have kids and not have nervous breakdowns when they do something like Caroline just did?" he asked.

"You cope with it, just the way you and Will and Ava did. You do whatever you can," Emma said.

"I'll never understand how you could stay cheerful and optimistic that we would find her. I know the reason you gave me, but I still don't get it"

"We did find her," she reminded him, sitting near him to sip her drink. He removed it from her hands and drew her down into his arms to kiss her. "I just try to focus on the positive, Zach. And Caroline hadn't been gone long when everyone started looking for her."

"I keep thinking she had reached the highway and if the Tanners hadn't come along—"

"But they did come along, so don't think about the other possibilities," Emma said. He held her in his embrace as they were stretched on the floor together. She had been frightened for Caroline, but certain they would find her. Now to know

Caroline was safe and with Will, Emma felt as if they had been given the biggest Christmas gift early.

Desire, relief, joy all buoyed her and she wrapped her arms around Zach to kiss him hungrily. Instantly, his arm tightened around her waist and he pulled her closer. "I need you tonight, Emma," he said in a rasp. "This is an affirmation of life and all's right with our world," he said, his blue eyes darkening as he drew her closer.

Seven

Relief transformed into lust, and loving Zach *was* an affirmation of life.

Heat from the fire warmed her, but not as much as Zach's kisses that sent her temperature climbing.

Sex with him became paramount. To be alive, to be able to make love with Zach, to have loved ones safe—her emotions ran high and she threw herself into kissing him, tangling her fingers in his thick hair.

She thought Zach was caught in the same emotional whirlwind, relieved, celebrating life and that all was okay now because his kisses became more passionate as he concentrated totally on pleasuring her.

In seconds they loved with a desperate hunger. With ragged breathing, she kissed him while her fingers traced muscles and planes of his body. Wild abandon consumed her and when they were joined, they rocked together until she cried out his name with her thundering release.

"Zach, ah, love," she gasped, the word slipping out and

she hoped he hadn't heard her. Rapture enveloped her, a moment in time when they were in unison and meant something to each other. A moment she wanted to hold, yet would be as fleeting as the snowflake she had caught and watched disappear in her warm palm.

Afterwards, as they drifted back to reality, he held her close in his arms while he showered her face and shoulders with light kisses that made her feel adored.

She turned on her side to look at Zach, drawing her fingers along his jaw to feel the rough, dark stubble. "This isn't what I expected tonight. Yet it's a rejoicing of sorts."

"A definite celebration of life for me." He sighed and traced his fingers over her bare shoulder. "I hope next week is another occasion for cheer. I have a doctor's appointment and I have high hopes I can get back into a normal shoe."

"When you do we'll be through here. Zach, I still urge you to keep those letters. You don't know if Caroline will want them one day. If you destroy them, you can't get them back."

"I know you've scanned most of them into the computer, so now we have electronic copies."

"The original letters are far more important."

He smiled. "Emma, you're a hopeless romantic. You're talking about letters written over a hundred years ago."

"I feel as if I know that part of your family. They were brave, intelligent and your great-great-grandfather had a sense of humor. I've found touching letters by your great-great-grandmother, too. I think the letters are priceless. And the fact that the letters date from over a hundred years ago has value, Zach. The electronic copies hold *no* value except they are copies if the originals are destroyed."

"I think you're placing too high a value on old letters. Now the things we've found mixed in with the letters, the gold watch, the Colt revolver, the Henry rifle—those are valuable. I can't believe someone put a Colt or a rifle in a box of letters."

"They put together what was important to them."

"No way are those letters as valuable as that Colt."

"Maybe not in dollars, but I think the letters are more valuable. The letters are a window into your ancestors' thoughts and dreams and lives."

He rose on an elbow to look at her. "We are polar opposites in every way. How can we possibly have this attraction that turns my insides out?"

"It does other things to you," she said, caressing him.

"You know what you're doing to me now," he said in a deep voice.

"Zach," she whispered, knowing the one part of their lives where they were totally compatible. "You're an incredibly sexy man," she added.

"That, darlin', is the pot calling the kettle black, as the old saying goes." His eyes darkened and his gaze shifted to her mouth as he leaned closer to kiss her.

She held him tightly while the endearment, his first, echoed in her mind and how she wished he had meant something by it. When it came to Zach, she couldn't hang on to that optimism she had everywhere else in her life.

Through the night they made love and slept in each other's arms. It was late morning before they dressed and ate. While Zach talked on the phone to Will, she sat at the kitchen table and gazed outside at the crystal blue swimming pool, the color reminding her of Zach's eyes. She thought about all she loved and admired about him—his generosity, his care for Caroline and his family, even if he didn't spend time with them, he obviously loved them. He was intelligent, talented, capable of running the businesses he owned and she had heard he started all of them, not his father. He was caring and fun, exciting, obviously a risk-taker although that wasn't a part that held high appeal for her.

As soon as he told Will goodbye, she stood. "Zach, I'm going back to work. I can still get a lot done today."

Nodding his head, he stood as she left the room. Her back tingled and she was tempted to turn around to stay with him and postpone work, but there was no point and no future in spending a lot of time with him. After this job ended, she did not expect to see him again.

Each day the rest of the week she spent nearly all her time reading the letters. When she returned Sunday night after the weekend at home, she was certain this would be her last week to work for Zach. A new concern nagged her constantly—for the first time, her period was late. They had used protection, so she dismissed the likelihood of pregnancy, but she didn't know what was wrong. Tuesday morning she called to make an appointment to see her family doctor the following week when she would be at home in Dallas.

Later that day, forgetting time or her surroundings, she read a yellowed letter on crackling paper.

"Zach, do you have a moment? Listen to this letter," she said. "This one is from your great-grandfather when their first child, a son, was born. Was your grandfather the oldest son?"

"Yes, he was," Zach said, leaning back in his chair.

She bent over the paper spread on her knees, her hair falling forward around her face.

"My dear sister. Lenore gave me a son today. He is a fine, strong baby and I am pleased. He has my color eyes and his mother's light hair. He has a healthy cry. I am certain his cries can be heard at the creek.

"With her long hair down Lenore looks beautiful. She has given me life's most precious gift. I feel humble, because there is nothing as valuable that I can present to her in return. I have done what I hope will please her the most. To surprise her I have ordered a piano for her.

"I wish I could give her fine satin gowns and a palace, but

she would merely laugh if I told her my wish. Instead, I hope she likes her piano. It will be shipped to Saint Joseph, Missouri, on the train. I will send four of the boys with a wagon and a team to go to Missouri to pick up the piano. They must protect it from the elements, thieves and all hazards because they will have to cross more than one treacherous river. They have promised they can get the piano and bring it back here."

Pausing, she looked up as Zach crossed the room to her. "Surely, that letter means something to you."

Taking the letter from her fingers to drop it back into the box, he pulled her to her feet, putting his arm around her waist. "I still say you're a romantic."

"If you destroy these, I think you'll have regrets."

"That's impossible for me to imagine. Today I'm filled with positive moments because I expect a great prognosis when I go to the doctor this afternoon. I think he'll say I'm healed and can wear regular shoes. After Christmas I want to take you dancing."

Her heart felt squeezed. She was thrilled while at the same time, that was only postponing their final parting.

"We'll see when the time comes," she said, placing her hands on Zach's chest. She could feel his heart beneath her palms and wondered if his reaction to her was half as strong as how he affected her. His blue eyes darkened with desire, causing her heartbeat to quicken. "You may not be able to dance as soon as you think. What is more likely—you'll be half a world away by that time."

"I don't think that's why you aren't accepting, is it?"

"I don't see much future for us. I think when you fully recuperate, you'll be gone. You'll return to life as you've always lived it. You have to agree."

"I might hang around Texas for a while. There are things I can do here. Wherever I am, I can fly home when I want to."

"I don't know how you can even call one place home."

This is the family ranch, now Garrett's, not your home. You don't stay in your home in Dallas," she argued breathlessly, having to make an effort to concentrate on their conversation when all she could think about was being in his arms and wanting him.

He smiled at her. "I'll ask again." Sparks arced between them, the air crackling. Just as it had been between them that first encounter, she was caught and held in his steady gaze that made her even more breathless.

"Zach," she whispered, sliding her arms around his neck.

He kissed her. Tingles streaked across her nerves. Awareness intensified of every inch of him pressed so close. Holding him tightly, she refused to think about the future, the job ending, her saying goodbye to Zach. Each day she was more in love with him. The world, work, letters, her future, all ceased to exist in her thoughts that focused totally on him.

His kiss turned her insides to jelly, ignited fires, heat sizzling in her. She pressed against him more firmly, taking what she could while he was here in her arms because too soon he would be gone forever.

Finally, she gave a thought to their time and place.

"Zach, there are other people in the house now," she whispered, wondering if her protests fell on deaf ears.

He kissed her, silencing her conversation. When she felt him tug on her sweater, she grasped his wrists. Breathing hard, he looked at her as she shook her head.

"We're downstairs. Nigel and Rosie are here. Within the hour you should leave for your flight to Dallas to see your doctor. We have to stop loving now."

Combing long strands of hair from her face, Zach looked at her mouth. "You're beautiful. We'll come back to this moment tonight when I get home."

"We shouldn't," she whispered. "You need to get lunch now before you go."

"I know what I'd rather do."

She shook her head. "Lunch is on the schedule."

"Ok, come eat with me." She nodded, walking beside him unable to resist. Through lunch he was charming, making her anxious for his return before he had even left the house

While he was gone the house was quiet and she read, stopping occasionally to stretch, or pacing the room and reading as she walked.

Late afternoon shadows grew long and she added a log to the fire. It was winter and the days had grown shorter with a chill in the air. She heard his whistle before he appeared When he came through the office door, he closed it behind him. Her heart thudded against her ribs. She took one look at him and knew her job was over.

Vitality radiated from him as if he had been energized while he was in Dallas. She didn't have to ask what the doctor had said. Zach crossed the room to pull her to her feet and kiss her heatedly

In minutes, clothes were tossed aside. The fire was glowing orange embers, giving the only light in the darkened room during early evening.

"Zach, we're downstairs and not alone in the house."

"The door is closed. No one will bother us," he whispered between kisses. "I want you, Emma." He kissed her before she could argue and she yielded, loving him back with a desperate urgency.

They moved to the rug in front of the fire. Heat warmed her side while Zach's body was hot against her own. He got a condom from a pocket and returned to kneel between her legs while he put it in place.

Orange sparks and embers highlighted the bulge of muscles and his thick manhood while the planes of his cheeks and flat stomach were shadows. Another memory to lock away in her mind and heart.

A log cracked and fell, sending a shower of sparks spiraling up the chimney. The sudden flash of red and orange dancing sparks illuminated Zach even more for a brief moment. He looked like a statue, power and desire enveloping him. She drew her fingers along his muscled thighs and heard him gasp for breath.

Lowering himself, he wrapped his arms around her to thrust slowly into her, filling her. He was hard, hot, moving with a tantalizing slowness as she arched beneath him.

"Zach," she whispered, wanting to confess her love, longing to hold him tightly and tell him she loved him with all her heart.

Their rhythm built, increasing need and tension, until release burst, spinning her into ecstasy, taking him with her seconds later.

She lost awareness of everything except Zach in their moment of perfect union. A physical bonding at the height of passion that carried with it an emotional bonding. Clinging to him with her long legs wrapped around him, she did not want to let go as if she could hold the moment and delay time itself. This man, so totally different from her, had become vital to her. Right now she couldn't face letting him go.

They slowed, calmed while she caught her breath. Her hands were light touches, caressing his shoulders and back while she drifted in paradise.

When he rolled over, taking her with him, he kissed her tenderly. There was still enough glow from embers to reflect on Zach and she touched his cheek lightly. "The doctor said your foot is healed, didn't he?"

"Yes, he did," Zach said, smiling. "I can toss this boot and wear my shoes. My own boots have to wait a while, but eventually, I can wear them."

"So my job ends this week. Christmas is coming and I wanted off anyway."

"I'll be gone for Christmas, but I'll come back afterwards and that's when I'm taking you out. I'd stay if you'd stay with me for a few weeks, but you'll want to be home for Christmas."

"Yes, I will," she said, hurting, even though she had known this time was approaching.

"I'll be in touch with you," he said. Glancing over his shoulder, he shifted away to stand and put another log on the fire. He returned to pull her close against him, warm body against warm body as he wrapped his legs with hers.

He combed her long hair away from her face with his fingers. Tingles followed each stroke and she could feel their hearts beating together.

"This is paradise, Emma."

How she longed to hear him say words of love. Common sense told her that would not happen, but wishes and dreams came with his strong arms holding her and his light kisses making her feel loved.

All were illusions that would disappear with the morning sun. For now she could pretend, wish, hope, give herself to fantasies that normally she wouldn't entertain for a minute.

She kissed him lightly in return.

The fire crackled and burned, causing dancing dark shadows and bathing Zach's body in orange.

"You're very quiet," he said.

"I'm savoring the moment."

"I'm savoring holding you close. Sometime tonight we'll get in a bed, but not yet."

Eventually, they gathered their clothing and each went to shower. They put away the dinner Rosie had cooked and made sandwiches to eat in front of the fire and sat and talked until Zach stood and took her hand.

"Let's go upstairs and I'll build a fire in my room. I can do stairs now with ease." He placed his arm across her shoulders as they climbed the stairs, leading her down the hall to his suite of rooms where he took her into his arms to kiss her.

Wednesday, she gave all her time to the letters. Zach's work had dwindled as Christmas approached, so since Thanksgiving she had devoted her time to trying to get through as many of the letters and memorabilia as she could.

She hoped someone else in the Delaney family wanted the letters because the few she had read to Zach and the ones he had read himself had not changed his feelings about them. He always sent them to the discard pile.

By Friday, the tension from being constantly around him—loving him, but not able to make him truly hers—was greater than ever. Today would change everything. Today she would return to Dallas, to her life before meeting Zach. Even though he had talked about seeing her after Christmas, she didn't expect to see Zach again.

Early that morning Rosie cooked while Emma ate breakfast. Halfway through breakfast, Emma felt sick and dashed to the bathroom. When she returned, she carried what was left of her breakfast back to the kitchen.

"Rosie, I can't eat any more. I felt sick and now food doesn't look good."

Rosie turned to study her while she dried her hands and took the dishes from Emma. "You were sick yesterday morning."

Emma looked at Rosie and met a speculative gaze. "My period is late," Emma said, confessing what had been worrying her each day. "I shouldn't be sick no matter what, but I am."

"Bless your heart," Rosie said, hugging Emma lightly. Emma stood immobile, stunned. Fear had blossomed earlier over a week ago. She had pushed away the nagging worry, telling herself it was her imagination. But it was too many days now for it to be her imagination. Two days in a row, she had been sick during breakfast and then it was gone.

"Rosie, I have two married sisters and a sister-in-law. They all have babies. I've seen both my sisters have morning sickness." Emma felt chilled and trembled. "Rosie, this wasn't in my plans."

"You don't know for certain, do you?"

"No. I'll get a pregnancy test this weekend when I go to Dallas. I already have a doctor's appointment for next week."

Rosie placed her hands on her hips while she faced Emma. "Then don't start worrying now. The stomach upset might be something you ate and your period could start tomorrow. How late are you?"

"A week now."

Emma rolled her eyes. "That's not enough to give you a worry. A few days is nothing. Wait a few weeks."

Emma nodded, but she was not reassured. "I'm extremely on time almost to the hour, so this is unique." Suddenly, to the depths, she was certain she was pregnant with Zach's baby. Her head swam and for an instant she felt light-headed. She reached out to grasp the kitchen counter to steady herself. Rosie's hand closed on her arm.

"Are you all right?"

Rosie's expression showed concern that threatened panic. "Rosie, promise me—please don't say anything yet until I know for sure."

"I would never. Don't give it another worry. That's not my business and I don't interfere in something like this. I'll not say anything." Rosie's brow furrowed and her eyes were filled with concern.

"I don't panic over things, but I feel panicky over this. I feel so out of control."

"Wait until you've seen a doctor and know absolutely," Rosie said, but her voice held only solicitude.

"This wasn't supposed to happen," Emma whispered, more to herself than Rosie.

"Some things are just out of our hands," Rosie declared. "Go back to your room and lie down if you need to." She took Emma's icy hand in her soft, warm hands, briefly and then released her. "You have a big, loving family. They'll take care of you and a little one."

A little one. Emma shook and clenched her hands. Rosie hadn't said a word about Zach being helpful. Was this going to be a huge shock—and an unpleasant one for him? Would it be a responsibility he didn't want? He had talked about how unprepared Will had been for Caroline. On the other hand, Zach seemed to truly care for Caroline and he had been a wreck when they couldn't find her. Of all men on earth— "I'm going to my room if he comes asking for me," she said, suddenly wanting to get behind closed doors and adjust to what was happening before she faced another person. "This is my last day. He doesn't need to know until I'm sure."

"I promise. You have your secret," Rosie said, nodding and going back to doing dishes.

Emma hurried out and raced out of sight, rushing to her room where she crossed the room to place her hands on her flat middle. "I can't be," she whispered.

In her dressing room she studied herself in the mirror, turning first one way and another. She had watched two sisters and a sister-in-law go through pregnancies. She looked in the mirror, running her hands over her flat stomach. There were no single mothers in her family.

Zach. How could she ever tell a man who wouldn't even spend Christmas with his family that he was about to become a father?

Eight

She was staring at her stomach in the dressing room of her suite when her stomach rolled and she ran for the bathroom. She was sick again and this time she knew it was partly with worry.

She thought of her brother, Connor. Connor was strong-willed, the take-charge oldest sibling, a total alpha male who would want to make Zach marry her. He wouldn't want to marry or he already would have talked about it. Zach would rebel and probably disappear to another country.

She shook again, chilled on the warm day. She ran a cold cloth over her face and went back to sit, knotting her fists and trying to think what to do, praying she was wrong.

She could leave, slip out without Zach even knowing and then say goodbye with a call from Dallas.

Too many things were so wrong. She had just tossed her future into uncertainty and chaos. Why had she ever stayed and worked for him? Why had she made love with him? Fallen in love with him when she had known it would be disastrous and hopeless? Why hadn't the protection worked?

The Dallas job would go, too. If she stayed there, word would get right back to him. *Just quit the company and go somewhere else,* she told herself. By the time she was ready to tell Zach, he would probably be halfway around the world, far from Texas and from her. Soon she would be only a memory to him.

Standing in front of the mirror, she inspected her figure. She could get through Christmas without anyone knowing. Common sense said to stop worrying until she was certain, but that was impossible. All her positive reactions to past upheavals were gone now. She couldn't hold the same cheerful certainty for herself and she needed to get a grip. This worry was not like her and there was a bright side. If she could just focus on the baby and try to avoid thinking about Zach. A total impossibility.

In her heart, there were no doubts. Because of their loving, she would become the mother of a Delaney. It seemed likely that Zach would help support his child, but that was all. A man whose heart was already given to traveling and his job would never be tied down by a family.

Feeling an ache of worry increasing, she rubbed her neck. Mary Kate was her closest sibling and she could tell her. The thought of Mary Kate's support lifted Emma's spirits slightly. Her sister would be a staunch ally and Emma was certain she could always count on her mother's acceptance. If she could just keep Connor from doing something wild like wanting to punch out Zach.

She remembered Will and Ava and Caroline and the love that shone between Will and Ava, plus their eagerness when they had announced a baby on the way. Emma hurt, her insides twisting into a knot while tears threatened. She wouldn't have that shared joy and love. This wasn't the way she had always dreamed about having a family. The love she had wished for was what she had witnessed between Will and Ava.

Emma wiped her eyes and got up, walking restlessly, wishing she could undo what had been done. She had no one to blame but herself. How she wished she could back up and relive her life.

Then Emma thought about the baby and put her hand protectively on her stomach. *Her* baby. Her family would be shocked, upset, angry, probably even with her, but when the baby arrived, they would all accept and love the tyke.

This baby would fit into her family and they would shower the baby and her with love. Her brothers would be dads for the baby. Her child would not come into the world unloved or unwanted.

She stretched on the bed, staring into space while her mind raced over problems and solutions.

The first hurdle was to get through today with Zach. She was already packed, ready to go home. How was she going to be able to tell Zach goodbye?

An hour later she went down to work. Zach sat stretched out, his feet on a window ledge while he talked on the phone. She sat at her desk, unable to work, looking at him and thinking about the future.

She could tell he was getting ready to end the call, so she returned to the box of letters where she had spent all of her time lately.

As she picked up a letter something rattled inside the envelope. Turning the envelope over, she shook it. A golden heart locket on a chain fell into her palm. Glittering brightly in the center of the heart was a brilliant green stone.

She withdrew the fragile letter and read, looking up to interrupt Zach. "Listen to this letter: '…this was my grandmother's locket with my great-grandmother's and my great-grandparents' pictures. I want you to have it because it should remain in the family to be passed to each generation.' This letter is signed by your great-grandfather, so this locket must be incredibly old if it belonged to his grandmother." Pausing, she put aside the letter. "Look at this beautiful locket. There are two tiny paintings inside with pictures, I suppose, of two more Delaneys, an even more distant generation." She carried the locket across the office to hand it to Zach.

Standing, he took the locket to turn it in his hand and inspect it.

Finally he looked up and held it out. "Emma, you take this. I want you to have it."

"Zach, I can't do that! You have a family and some of your relatives may want it. You should keep that jewelry. It's an heirloom and your great-grandfather wanted it to stay in the Delaney family."

"You said you feel as if you are part of the Delaneys when you read those old letters. I want you to have it as a bonus for your work and to give you a tangible memory of all this history you waded through. Here," he said, taking it from her and stepping behind her to fasten it around her neck.

"I really think you should keep this in your family," she said and then realized part of her would become part of his family. She placed her fist protectively against her stomach.

"I want you to have it," he insisted, taking her shoulders to turn her to face him as he judged how it looked on her. "It is pretty," he added, his voice deepening while it thickened with desire. He looked into her eyes. She met his blue ones, her heart beating faster. She wanted his strong arms around her. She wanted to hold him while she kissed him. As if he could read her thoughts, he drew her to him and placed his mouth on hers.

Her heart slammed against her ribs. Zach pulled her close, holding her tightly while he kissed her hard and possessively.

Her pounding heart should indicate her feelings as she

held him tightly in return. She let go all restraint, kissing him, her deepest love, the father of her baby. And she was certain she was pregnant. How she wished she didn't ever have to tell him.

"Zach," she said, on the verge of saying she would miss him. "Thank you for the necklace. Your brothers and your half sister may not be happy with you for giving away this heirloom."

"My brothers would definitely want you to have it. Sophia, I don't know. I want you to have it. Actually, I don't think I'm making you much of a gift except I suspect you think so.".

She looked at the locket in her hand and got a knot in her throat as emotions choked her. "I do think so," she whispered, knowing it would go to a Delaney heir.

Zach put his finger beneath her chin to raise her face. Embarrassed because she couldn't hide her emotional reaction, she stood on tiptoe and kissed him quickly.

As their kiss became passionate, her emotions shifted. When she ended their kiss, they both were breathless and she suspected Zach had forgotten about her reaction to the locket.

"I'm going to miss you, Emma."

"You can still come spend Christmas with us," she said, certain of his answer.

He smiled. "Thanks, but I've already made arrangements. I'll be at an Italian villa I inherited. Dad always referred to it as his 'summer home.'"

His answer stung and made her leaving a reality. Yet it was for the best because now her emotions were on a rocky edge. They needed to part even though she felt as if her heart were breaking.

She placed her hand against his cheek. "I'll think about you on Christmas in your Italian villa."

"You are probably the one person in the entire world who

feels sorry for me spending Christmas that way," he said, smiling at her.

"I know what you're missing."

"We can both say that. You could come with me and let me show you that Italian villa and see how you like spending Christmas in Italy. Live a little, you have next Christmas with your family."

"Thank you, but I'll stay in Texas and you go to Italy. Zach, you get along with your family—your brothers and Caroline mean a lot to you. Realize what a treasure they are. Love and enjoy them. I think you shut yourself off in defense when you were hurt as a child. You have a wonderful family and your ancestors are fascinating. Don't sell them short. Try a Christmas with Will and family sometime, get Ryan, Sophia and Garrett there, too."

"You are a dreamer and a romantic," he said patiently. "I will enjoy my Italian villa immensely. It will be sunny, beautiful with no crowds, no schedules. You really should try it."

She shook her head. "Thank you. We'll each go where our hearts are, only I think yours is there out of an old habit more than because you really enjoy it."

"I suppose I never stopped to think about it."

She stepped away and glanced at her watch. "I need to get on the road now. The job has been wonderful." She tried to hold back tears as she stood on tiptoe to kiss him.

He held her tightly, kissing her fiercely. Finally, he paused. "You can stay this weekend if you want."

"I have plans in Dallas," she said, knowing it would be heartbreaking to spend the weekend and go through this last day again.

She stepped out of his embrace. It was time to go. She'd already said her goodbyes to Rosie and Nigel, and Nigel had already placed her things in her car.

Zach headed out with her, reaching around her to open the car door.

"You'll hear from me," he said.

"Maybe I'll see you at headquarters someday," she replied lightly, sliding behind the wheel. Closing the door, he stepped back and she started the car. As she waved and drove away, she glanced in the rearview mirror to see him standing in the drive, watching her.

She would tell her mother and sisters she had been invited to Zach's Italian villa. Connor didn't need to hear about it. An Italian villa sounded like paradise, but not at Christmas. That was definitely family time.

Family time. Worry and heartbreak stung. She couldn't keep from crying until she thought about the baby and making plans. How and when would she tell her family? She'd wait until after Christmas because she had no idea how they would receive the news.

Zach had seemed good with Caroline and interested in her. How would he be with his own child? He had told her how they had struggled to get Sophia into the family and how much they wanted to know her. Surely, if he wanted to know his half sister, he would want to know his child.

The first thing was to get a pregnancy test kit. If she wasn't pregnant, then all these worries would seem ridiculous.

Pregnant—it was a shock she couldn't absorb. It was so totally unexpected because they had always used protection. Something she had never thought would happen to her until after she was married. She had always looked forward to her own family, but in her mind, it had included a husband who was an active family man. A reassuring thought now was the knowledge she would never be alone raising this baby because her family would all participate. Clinging to that, she tried to ignore the steady hurt squeezing her heart.

Christmas with a baby on the way. Would she have to give

up college and her hope of teaching? Christmas had always been filled with magic for her, the best time of the year, and this Christmas would be so different. She would have to be responsible for someone else. It was an awesome task. She would get a present for her baby this week. And think of baby names. Her baby would not have the Delaney name. Another Hillman.

She missed Zach. As mismatched as they were, she liked being with him. He had been easy to work for. When she decided what and how she would tell him about the baby, she would get in touch with him. In the meantime, this break was as inevitable as it was necessary.

She fingered the locket around her neck. She thought it was a beautiful heirloom and she would take very good care of it. It would go into safekeeping for her baby soon.

She hoped Will prevailed on Zach to keep the letters. It would be sad to see them destroyed. Since she would be mother of a Delaney, if they decided to shred the letters, she intended to ask Zach for them.

She missed Zach badly and each mile between them increased her longing to be with him. She could have prolonged the separation, but there was no point and her emotions were on a raw edge. In a few hours she would be home and her family would keep her busy enough that the pain over parting with Zach should be alleviated.

By Monday, Zach missed Emma more than he had thought possible. He was planning to leave for Italy on Tuesday, but he had lost his enthusiasm for the trip. Should he do something else this Christmas? That was Emma's influence. He recalled times as a child that he had wanted to be with his family, but then he and his brothers had been left at their schools for the holidays. Eating at the home of an indifferent headmaster had never been fun and Zach began to count only on his own company. He would be happy in Italy once he was there.

Earlier that morning Will had called his brothers and Sophia, and the entire family was coming for lunch today to bring their Christmas presents to him, so he was having a little Christmas celebration with his family. Emma would have been relieved to hear it, but now she was wrapped up in her own family's activities. When he first was injured, Zach had given his secretary at headquarters a list of gifts to purchase for each member of his family. They'd been wrapped and delivered to the ranch.

Standing at the window, Zach looked at the dry, yellowed windswept landscape beyond the fenced yard. Why had life become empty without Emma? It had only been the weekend since she left, but it seemed eons ago. Common sense told him she was not the woman for him, not even in a casual way. He smiled at the thought. No relationship was casual to Emma. Not even the brief affair they had.

He paced the room restlessly. "Go to Italy," he advised aloud. "Pick up your life and forget her."

Memories flooded him of holding her, kissing her, making love to her. Of her laughter, her hands on him, her luminous green eyes studying him. Even the looks of pity she had given him came back to haunt him. Was he missing out on the best part of life as she had said? Was he letting that armor from childhood keep him from loving and being loved today?

Would he really want to be tied down with a family? Tied down with Emma? The last thought sounded like paradise.

Was he going to mope through Christmas? It was a time he had never given much thought to since he was grown.

He saw three limos coming up the drive so he left to open the front door.

Will, Ava and Caroline climbed out of the first limo. Ryan emerged from the second and Garrett and Sophia from the third limo. The drivers carried boxes filled with wrapped presents. Zach directed the drivers where to put the presents and then turned to greet everyone.

"Don't tell me all this stuff is for me," Zach said.

"Who else is here for us to give presents to? Although I do have one for Nigel and one for Rosie and I'll bet the rest do, too," Ryan said with a cocky grin. "You said you were giving Nigel and Rosie three weeks off."

"And I did. Come in," he said, picking up Caroline to give her a hug. He led them to the family room where the drivers had already placed boxes of presents.

A sofa beside a large wingback chair was piled high with Zach's presents for his brothers, Sophia and their families.

"You should have had Nigel bring down the Christmas tree," Will said.

"Don't you start that. Emma had decorations up and I got rid of them."

"You have turned into Scrooge," Will said.

"Hardly," Zach replied, waving his arm in the direction of the sofa with presents. "I believe I have a few presents for everyone."

"My apology," Will said, laughing. "Not entirely Scrooge. I do see mistletoe hanging over the door. That's a weird decoration to put up for a man living alone."

"Just drop it, Will," Zach said.

"Maybe I should have stopped by last week and met the secretary," Ryan said.

"Will a beer shut you two up?" Zach asked. "First, let me see about the drivers and get them settled with something to eat and drink. I'll be right back. When I do, we'll start this little family Christmas celebration that I suspect is totally for my benefit," Zach remarked dryly.

When he returned he asked them, "Eggnog, beer, wine, martini, margaritas, Scotch, an old-fashioned—none of you have to drive home and I have a full bar, so what do you prefer?" he said, going behind the bar to fill orders. In minutes he brought out snacks Rosie had left.

Ryan held up his bottle. "Merry Christmas to our newest family member, Sophia, to Ava and Caroline, to my big brothers, to Garrett who's been like a brother," he said, including Garrett as he always had.

They all held up bottles and echoed his toast.

"Now I'll propose a toast," Will said, "and a Christmas prayer of thanks for Caroline in our lives, for Sophia becoming part of our family and for Ava. The four of us have been blessed by them."

"Here, here and amen," Ryan said and they clinked bottles together again.

In a few minutes Ryan raised his bottle high again. "Here's to the two surviving bachelors in this group. Zach, my bro, I'm going to outlast you."

All three of the others protested at the same time. "Ryan, you're next," Garrett said. "No way is anyone getting Zach down the aisle."

"They can't get him to stay in one country long enough to fall in love," Will added, making Zach grin.

"Sorry, Ryan, but I'll win this one," he said, thinking about Emma.

They soon went to the kitchen where Zach got out ribs from a Dutch oven. All night he had cooked ribs and he had baked beans that had slowcooked for hours. He got a large bowl of Rosie's cold potato salad. He replenished beers and they all gathered around the big table to feast on the rib dinner. As he passed out the beers, he thought of Emma. If she could see him now, she would know he enjoyed his family. They just weren't together as often as hers.

"When are you leaving for Italy?" Will asked.

"Tomorrow. The weather prediction is good. So when is everyone else going?"

"We're leaving tomorrow morning for Colorado," Will replied. "Caroline is hyped over going and she is almost climbing the walls now," he said, smiling at her and Caroline giggled.

"Garrett, when do you leave?"

"We'll go to my folks' house Thursday. We're going out with Sophia's friends Friday night."

"Ryan, what about you?"

"I'm leaving to go back to Houston. I need to see if I still have a drilling business, I've been gone so long. Meg and I have parties Friday night, Saturday night and Sunday night. Meg's a party girl."

"Meg?" Zach asked. "Should I know who Meg is?"

"No. I can answer for him," Will said. "Meg is just the most recent." He grinned at Ryan. "You two are kids, still doing kid stuff," Will teased.

"May be kid stuff, but it's fun. At least I'm not so decrepit I have to sit around someone's home each of those nights," he teased.

"And Zach in Italy. Who is the latest beautiful lady?"

"I'll be alone at my villa, which is fine."

"Well, all of you should come to Colorado. This is going to be the best ever Christmas," he said, smiling at Ava and then at Caroline. "We have a Santa suit for Muffy that Caroline thinks Muffy loves to wear. We'll have worlds of fun and if anyone wants to come afterwards to ski and enjoy Colorado, you're invited. Except our invalid."

"Not an invalid any longer," Zach said. "Doc's given me a big okay and I can do whatever I want. We didn't discuss skiing."

"C'mon, Zach," Ryan said. "Garrett, you, too. Let's fly

up there after Christmas and ski. I'll come, Will, right after
New Year's if you're staying that long."

"Sure. All of you come join us. You can bring anyone you
want with you."

"I'll see how it goes in Italy," Zach said. "I doubt if I'll be
back that soon."

"The bird has flown the coop again," Will teased. "You
just can't stay put. We'll see you next summer."

"I'll pass this time, but thanks," Garrett said. "I'm building furniture and Sophia is painting."

"Still the workaholic," Ryan stated. "Some things never
change."

They ate ribs until they had a platter filled with bones.
When they finished, they all cleaned up and soon they returned to the family room to open gifts.

The first gift went to Caroline and her eyes sparkled as she
unwrapped a box that held a new doll. She gave Zach a hug
and he smiled at her. "Merry Christmas, sweetie," he said,
wishing Emma was with him.

After the gifts were unwrapped and stacked neatly to go,
Zach said he had something else for them.

He left and returned with a box holding the gold pocket
watch, the Colt revolver and the Henry rifle. "My secretary
and I have been through a lot of the memorabilia. I don't
know why these things were buried under the letters. So far,
we found these three items. Why doesn't each family take
one. We can draw if you want to see who gets what, regarding this stuff."

"You ought to have something," Garrett said. "Leave me
out. These are Delaney possessions and I'm not a Delaney."

"Sophia is," Zach said immediately. "There was a locket
that I gave to my secretary. Sorry, I didn't wait to ask you,
Sophia, when I gave Emma the necklace. She has pored over

this stuff and enjoyed it. You'd think these people were related to her."

"That's fine, Zach," Sophia said. "Really. I don't need it and it's nice you gave it to her."

"Sophia, you participate," Zach said. "I'm staying out of it because all of you know I don't care about the letters and the ancestors and our past. It's history."

"Our parents weren't sentimental, and you're really a chip off the old block," Will said.

"Now that remark and comparison, I can do without." Zach scribbled out words on three pieces of paper and wadded each up. "We can draw or you can each say what you want and see if anyone else wants it. Or we can go in order of age."

"Hand us the papers and that will be that," Will said.

Zach held out his hand and in seconds Will picked up the Henry rifle, Ryan the Colt revolver and Sophia the pocket watch. "Okay. Is everyone happy with what you got?" Zach asked.

"Sure," Ryan said, rubbing his hand along the Colt. "This is excellent."

"I love this watch—more than I would the rifle or the revolver," Sophia said. "I would like one of the letters to put with it."

"Good choice. I like the watch," Garrett said, exchanging a smile with his wife.

"Go to the office and pick out whatever letters you want," Zach instructed. "We can divide them all three ways when someone finishes going through them."

"These things are treasures," Ryan said, continuing to turn the revolver in his hand.

"The Henry rifle is fantastic. I'm definitely happy," Will added.

It was late afternoon when Garrett stood. "We need to get home because we're flying back to Dallas."

Ryan stood and gathered his gifts. "I'll go, too. Soon I'll fly out for a tropical paradise, palm trees and warm breezes and a beautiful woman."

"Won't seem like Christmas," Will said. "Of course, you may not care. I'll bet you'll be ready for snow-covered mountains before New Year's."

"Probably will," Ryan replied cheerfully.

"You can bring your friend with you."

Ryan winked. "I think I'll come alone and see if I can find a new friend. See you in the summer, Zach, and thanks."

"You're welcome. I'll let your drivers know you're going."

Zach saw them out, then returned to join Will and Ava while Caroline played with her new doll. "Want one more beer? You don't have to go because they did."

"Sure, I'll have a beer. Is your foot hurting?"

"No. It's healed," Zach said, getting two beers from the bar.

"You don't look so great. Anything worrying you?"

"No. Maybe you're getting me mixed up with Ryan. He's the one who's always got a smile. Remember, I don't have his rosy outlook on life. This is my natural look all the time."

"I know that, but you aren't usually as quiet as today and you look as if something's on your mind besides Christmas and us."

"Actually, Christmas hasn't been on my mind, which I'm sure, surprises no one. "

"What do you think about the prospects for the Cowboys this next year?"

"Great," Will answered and the talk shifted to football and then moved to business while they told each other what the current projects were.

When Ava and Will finally stood to go, he paused. "Will you come back from Italy or just go to a job site?"

"Probably just go to a site. I'm through here, so I'm dump-

ing the letters and memorabilia. It's up to you and Ryan now.
Garrett, too, if you can rope him into it because of Sophia."

"I'll see. So you sent your secretary back to the Dallas
office."

"Yes. We won't see each other again. She turned out to be
efficient and good, Will. She's read a mountain of old letters."

"I don't want to shred them. She's right about a tie to our
past."

"With time they'll disintegrate. She copied some of them
carefully and put them in a scrapbook between clear acid-
free sheets. She said that way we can make copies for family
members who want them."

"I'm astounded they got through our parents without being
destroyed. You know Mom wouldn't care at all about them.
Dad didn't until the end of his life."

"Frankly, I can't work up a lot of interest."

Will chuckled. "So how did she get you to go home for
Thanksgiving with her? Is there something going on here
that I haven't been told?"

"Will, don't quiz your brother about his personal life," Ava
said, smiling at Will. "Caroline and I will say goodbye. The
ribs were delicious and thank you for the gifts. You know
we'll all love everything."

"Merry Christmas, Ava," Zach said, walking her and Caroline outside. "Take care of him."

"Merry Christmas, Zach. I intend to," she answered and
waited while he hugged Caroline before the two of them
climbed into the limo to wait for Will.

"So how did your secretary get you to go home for Thanksgiving with her?" Will persisted.

"I think she's trying to rescue me. You can't imagine how
sorry she feels for me and how much sympathy I get."

"Sympathy." The word burst from Will and he started
laughing. "She feels sorry for you because you don't celebrate

these holidays. Does she know how you live and how much money you spend whooping it up on holidays?"

Zach grinned as he shook his head.

"So she made you go home with her for Thanksgiving. Now what in the world incentive did she use to get you to do that?"

"Mind your own business, Will. And the best possible incentive of all."

"I never ever thought I'd see the day."

"You haven't seen it yet. Don't worry, there isn't anything serious between us and there won't be. She is one hundred percent a homebody. I'm almost one hundred percent traveler. That's not a good fit and we both know it."

"Yeah, right," Will said, smiling. "By the way, you didn't tell me that she's gorgeous. I know now why from the first you didn't want me to get someone else to work for you."

"She's an efficient secretary."

"With drop-dead looks. Well, merry Christmas," Will said, impulsively hugging his brother. Startled Zach hugged Will in return.

"I think Caroline and Ava are changing you," Zach said, stepping back. "It's a good change, Will. None of us wanted to turn out to be like Dad."

"Sure as hell not. He was as cold as ice until Caroline came along. She'll never know how she has affected this family."

"All for the better and you're good for her."

"I'm trying. Ava's the one."

"It's you, too. Don't sell yourself short," he said following Will to the limo door. The driver held it. "Merry Christmas, Will. Thanks for my presents."

Zach stepped back and watched as the driver closed the door and went around to get behind the wheel. He continued watching the limo go down the drive, but his thoughts were on Emma. Tomorrow he was scheduled to leave for a night in New York and then to Italy. Right now, he didn't feel in-clined to leave Texas. This was home more than Italy. He was comfortable here. He had to admit, he was a lot closer here to Emma than he would be in Italy. If he just had to see her, he could in only a few hours' time. From Italy, it would be a real trek.

Jamming his hands into his pockets, he went back to the empty house. How could it seem so big and empty with Emma gone? What was she doing at this moment? Did she miss being with him?

Inside, he closed the front doors and heard the locks click in place. He stood in the entryway and debated whether to call her. It was pointless, so he went to the office, pausing beneath the mistletoe. He reached up to take down the deco-ration, turning it in his hands, remembering her kisses. Sex with Emma had been the best ever. Of all women, Emma was the only one who had created sparks the first moment they looked at each other. She definitely was the only one to include him in her family gatherings, the only one to make him rethink his past, the only one he had ever really missed.

With a sigh he tossed the mistletoe on a table. He didn't expect her to be back at the ranch ever.

He didn't want to go to New York tomorrow. He picked up his cell to tell his pilot they weren't going until later in the week. He didn't have to be anywhere at any specific time so there was no rush to leave Texas.

Tuesday afternoon he didn't feel any more inclined to leave for New York and Italy than he had on Monday. Even with-out Emma, he would rather be at the ranch than in an empty house in Italy. He didn't want to ruin his pilot's Christmas, just because he didn't care about his own, so he told his pilot he would stay in Texas until after the holiday. If he decided to go, he could catch a commercial flight. Or just go to New York and spend Christmas there.

Feeling glum, he reached for his phone to call Emma just to talk. How many times he had done that the past few days, and then decided he wouldn't call her?

He was restless and nothing interested him. Emma occupied his thoughts most of his waking hours.

Startling him, he received a call on his cell phone. Shaking his head, he was tempted to not answer when he saw it was from Will. Afraid it would be an emergency, he said hello.

"Zach, it's Will. Where are you? Italy or Texas?"

Zach swore and gritted his teeth. Will usually didn't call until Christmas day. "I'm still in Texas, but will go to Italy soon."

"I just thought you might still be in Texas. What's wrong?" Will asked.

"There's nothing wrong. Staying here is just easier."

"Right," Will said. "Could it be that you miss Emma? I imagine she invited you to spend Christmas with her family. You could, you know," Will said without giving Zach time to answer his question.

"I am not spending Christmas with Emma and sixty other Hillmans."

"So then pack and go to Italy. You'll forget her and get over her."

"Thanks. I plan to go to Italy. I'm just not in a rush," he said, thinking he wasn't going to get over Emma anytime soon.

"Well, I know it's a safe bet you haven't fallen in love, so I'll stop worrying about you. You can still fly up here if you want. Caroline will take your mind off Emma. Caroline is having a blissful time. Christmas is magical for her and she's turning it into magic for us."

"That's great, Will," Zach said with sincerity.

"Even Muffy is enjoying the snow. We have to clear paths

for her or she'll sink out of sight. Give some thought to join-
ing us."

"Thanks. Bye, Will," Zach said and ended the call without
giving Will a chance to prolong it.

Zach returned to staring at smoldering logs in his fireplace
while Emma filled his thoughts. Did she miss him or was
she immersed in family Christmas activities? He held up his
phone, tempted to call her, finally giving in to the temptation.

At first he thought she wasn't going to answer, but then he
heard her voice and his heart skipped beats.

"Zach, you're calling from Italy?"

"I haven't gone yet. I'm going to New York first," he said.
"Ready for Christmas?"

"Hardly, but I will be soon. Something's always going on
around here. People coming over or someone wanting me to
do something or Mom needs help. I'm busier than ever. Have
you heard from Will or Ryan?"

"Will today. They're having a great time," he said, longing to be with her. The phone call only made him miss her
more and he felt ridiculous for calling. "I'll have to admit,
the place seems empty with you gone."

There was a long silence. "I miss being there."

"No, you don't, really," he said, smiling, certain she didn't,
but he hoped she missed him.

"I do miss you," she said solemnly in a quiet voice that
made his heart lurch. He inhaled deeply, wanting her with
him, in his arms now.

"Will you go out with me for New Year's Eve? I'll come
home if you will."

There was another long pause and he held his breath.
"Yes," she said. "The sensible part of me says no and I'm
sure you feel the same."

"We'll have a good time," he said lightly, his heart racing
with eagerness that he would see her again and go out with

her. He settled back to talk, asking about her family, enjoying listening to her, glad for this tenuous connection that was still a link with her.

They talked for over an hour before Emma broke in. "Zach, my family is calling me. I promised I'd go shopping and they're waiting for me to join them."

"Sure. See you New Year's," he said.

The connection ended and he felt more alone than he had in years. He wanted Emma with him. How could she have taken such a place in his life that he couldn't get along without her now?

New Year's Eve seemed an eternity away. He stretched and walked around restlessly. He couldn't concentrate on work. He didn't want to go to Italy. He didn't want to join Will because all he would do was think about Emma.

He left to head for his gym while he stayed lost in thought about her.

Emma hurried out to join her sisters and mother to spend the afternoon shopping, but the entire time, she couldn't keep Zach out of mind. She was going out with him for New Year's Eve. Surprise had been her first reaction. She was astounded he wanted to pursue a relationship. She had debated only a moment with herself. Now that she was carrying his baby, everything had changed. Whether she or Zach liked it or not, she would be tied to him for years. Unless he totally rejected his child and she didn't think he would. Not when he seemed to care so much for his niece. She still couldn't accept having a casual relationship with him, but she would just have to see how he reacted and what he wanted.

The aching gloom that had enveloped her when she parted with him had lifted, leaving only worry•over his reaction to her news. Excitement, joy over the prospect of an evening with him was tinged with concern over when and how to break the news to him about their baby. If he rejected this child, he would break her heart. Even though he had rejected her lifestyle and hadn't wanted her in his life permanently, this baby was more important now and life had changed.

By five in the afternoon, she was exhausted from shopping and wanted to go home and take a nap. She suspected her mother might be wearing down also, so she told Mary Kate she thought they should call it a day.

It was almost six before they actually unloaded the car and were settled back at home. Emma headed to her room, leaving her packages to get later. All she wanted to do was stretch out and get a quick snooze.

She hadn't been in bed five minutes when there was a knock on her door and Mary Kate appeared.

"Can I talk to you a minute?" she asked, stepping into the bedroom and closing the door. She shook her dark brown hair away from her face as she crossed the room. Her tan sweater emphasized gold flecks in her hazel eyes.

"Sure, come in. Does Mom need help with dinner?"

"No, she's lying down, too, and Sierra has gone home with her brood. So has Lynne to relieve Connor of watching their kids. They all promised to come back after a while." Mary Kate sat on the edge of the bed.

"You've got all the energy," Emma remarked.

"How are you feeling?"

"Tired. We did a lot of shopping and I guess the work I've been doing and the Christmas stuff has caught up with me. I'm sleepy."

"Sure. You were sick this morning when I came."

Emma sat up slightly. "Whatever it was, it passed."

"You know I'm here for you," Mary Kate said, her hazel eyes filled with concern and Emma took a deep breath.

"How did you know?" Emma asked, certain her sister had guessed she was pregnant.

Nine

Mary Kate shrugged. "I've been there," she said, tugging up the sleeves of her tan sweater.

Emma sat up. "You haven't been there as a single mom. Not in this family. MK," she said, reverting to the nickname, "I don't know what I'm going to do." she said. Tears threatened and she tried to get a grip on her emotions.

Mary Kate hugged her and Emma clung tightly to the sister who had stood by her through so many childhood scrapes.

As she released her sister, Emma wiped her eyes. "This was unplanned, unexpected and shouldn't have ever happened. I'm carrying Zach's baby."

"Zach Delaney. Boy, you picked one. That's what I was afraid of. Does he know?"

"No, not yet."

"Do you have any idea how he will react?"

"Not really. He seems crazy about his niece, but he's taken no responsibility for her. When her father was killed, Zach's older brother became guardian. Zach is solitary, a total loner and happy in that life. He rarely comes home. He works abroad, all over the world and loves what he does. He doesn't need the money. He travels to dangerous places and he likes it."

"I thought I heard you say he's in demolition."

"Yes. His company has other businesses, but that's the one he loves and takes an active part in. A big active part. That's how he hurt his foot. Somehow, I can't see him taking this well at all. He doesn't have serious relationships. I wonder if he goes out much because of his lifestyle. He keeps to himself and spends holidays alone, including Christmas."

"Christmas—alone? Through his own choice?"

"Yes."

Her sister's frown reflected her own feelings about Zach's view of holidays. "Wow. Well, even if he has nothing to do with you or the baby, you have a family who will be right with you."

"If Connor doesn't try to punch Zach."

Mary Kate laughed. "He won't. Connor grumbles, but he's too much like Dad to resort to fists unless someone else starts something. Do you think Zach will give you any financial support?"

"I'm guessing he will, but I don't know. If he doesn't offer, I'm not pursuing it. I'll manage and he paid me extravagantly for the job I just did, plus I have a good job with his company and money saved. I'll manage."

"I'm sure you will," Mary Kate said, shifting to a more comfortable seat on the side of the bed. "What about your education and a teaching job? That's what you've always wanted."

"I think that will have to be postponed," Emma said. "I'll use this money for the baby. Later on, I hope I can pick up where I left off, go back to college, get my degree and then teach."

"I hope Zach Delaney does what's right and gives you financial support. Marriage sounds like an unlikely event."

"It's impossible. He's totally solitary. MK, how will I tell Mom and Dad? It's Dad I'm worried about. I think this will break his heart. And I know—I should have thought of that before now."

"You're not getting a lecture from me. Dad's able to take news and he'll help you and so will Mom. I know it's hard to think about telling them, but don't worry about it. Just do it and get it over with."

"I'm waiting until after Christmas and you wait, too."

Mary Kate ran her fingers over her lips. "Absolutely. This is your deal to tell the family, not mine. I'm just here for you. And don't expect it to be long before Mom catches on. She's been through this five times."

"I know."

I better go see what the kiddos are doing. Bobby's watching them and he's as much a kid as they are. Holler if you want to talk again."

"Thanks, MK."

"Sure."

Emma settled back against pillows and watched her sister leave the room. She could count on MK. Actually, she could count on her whole family. It was just Zach who was an unknown factor.

She thought about New Year's Eve. That would be the time to break the news. As soon as Christmas had passed she would tell the family.

She missed Zach. How long would she continue to miss him? Months, years, forever?

Christmas Eve morning, Zach sat at his desk trying to think about work and finding it impossible. Emma dominated his thoughts every waking hour. He hadn't gone to Italy and he still didn't want to go. He wouldn't do any more in Italy than he would on the ranch, so he just stayed. He felt closer to Emma here and the house reminded him of moments she had been there. How many times during the week had he pulled out his phone and started to call her?

He tossed his pen and rubbed the back of his neck. He wanted to see her and he was tired of trying to think about work and failing completely.

The phone rang and he saw the caller ID indicated Will, which was no surprise. Zach was tempted to avoid answering and the questions that would follow. Taking a deep breath, he picked up his phone to talk.

"Yes, Will, I'm here at the ranch. I decided to stay in Texas." He tried to put some cheer in his voice and realized he was failing.

"Are you sick?"

"No, I'm not."

"Is Rosie there?"

"No. You know I gave her and Nigel three weeks off. I'm okay. Merry Christmas. Let me talk to Caroline."

He talked briefly to his niece and she suddenly said goodbye and Will returned. "We're getting snow. How's the weather there?"

"I know you didn't call to get a weather report."

"No, I didn't. Just some small talk while I walked into an-other room and closed the door for privacy. Zach, if you're in love with Emma, do something about it. You might have to live life a little more on the ordinary side like the rest of us do."

Zach had to laugh. "And a merry Christmas to you, too, Dr. Phil. Stop giving me advice."

"Okay, but this is so unlike you. Do you want to fly up here today and spend tomorrow with us? I promise we're fun."

"I'm sure you're fun galore, but I'm happy here," he said,

giving some thought to Will's invitation. For the first time he was slightly tempted, but he still preferred Texas where he was closer to Emma. "When have I not been happy alone?"

"Maybe since you met Emma Hillman. Well, you're a grown man and I won't give you advice, just an invitation. And a merry Christmas."

"Thanks, Will. Thanks for calling and for your invitation. I really mean it. Merry Christmas to you all."

As he hung up, Zach had to smile over his brother's ridiculous call. He paced restlessly and then stopped to look down at the largest box of memorabilia. He pulled up a chair and picked up a letter to read.

"All right, Emma. I'll try again to find something fascinating in my ancestors' lives."

He read two letters and tossed both in the discard box. He picked up another and saw it was his written by his great-great-grandfather during the second year of the Civil War.

"My dearest Tabitha:

"My love, we covered twenty miles today in the rain. It is dark and cold now and I write by firelight. I am glad we did not encounter any of our enemy because our ammunition and our supplies run low. I am fortunate to have both my rifle and my revolver, plus ammunition. Others are not so fortunate. This ghastly war between the States is tearing our country apart. My dearest, how I miss you! If I could just hold you against my heart. You and our son.

"This fighting is lonely and desperate. How I long to be with you this night and see your smile, that would be a Christmas treasure to me. Know that I send my love to you on this Christmas night. You and our little one are the most important part of my life and what I am fighting for. I dream of peace for our babe and his descendants and their offspring. How I wish I could see our son, this precious babe. My heart aches with wanting to be with you and my child on this night.

*Nothing else on this earth matters, but I fight to keep life se-
cure for the two of you."*

For the first time Zach felt a thread of kinship with this
ancestor from generations earlier. Feeling foolish for his
emotional reaction to the old letter, Zach continued to read.
*"I close my eyes and imagine you holding out your arms
and smiling at me. Someday, my love, we will be together
again. Know that I send my love to you and our son on this
Christmas night."* He could be saying those words to Emma.
Leaning back in his chair, Zach watched flames dance in the
fireplace. He missed Emma. He could imagine the ache in
his relative's life on a cold Christmas night away from his
young wife and a baby.

He picked up the letter to continue reading:

*"Know you are my life and you and our offspring have my
love always. I want this land to be safe for our son and his
sons. My family I hold dearest of everything on this earth. I
dream of when I can come home and we are together once
again. My love, how I long to hold you close to my heart. All
my love to you from your adoring husband, Warner Irwin
Delaney."*

Zach had a tightening in his chest and he placed the letter
in the discard box with the others without thinking about what
he was doing. As he finished reading, all his thoughts focused
on Emma and the letter. She would have been touched by it.

Was he missing out on life as she had said? Was he missing
the most treasured part—a woman's love and a family's love?

He had never really thought marriage could be happy and
filled with love until he had been with Emma's family, because he had never seen a loving family in his own home or
his oldest brother's or even in any of his friends. Garrett's
parents seemed the closest and Garrett had been happy growing up, but the Cantrells had not exhibited the warmth and
closeness the Hillmans had.

Will had not been married long enough for his marriage to count. Will was in euphoria and still steeped in his honeymoon. The Hillman seniors had been married for years and they were obviously in love. Zach had never thought of marrying or having a child—yet he loved Caroline and he barely saw her. How much more would he love one of his own that he saw often? Surely he would love his offspring deeply, and, if he ever had any, he intended to give them all the time and attention he possibly could.

Emma was a steadying influence, her calm faith in love, her cheer, her optimism—maybe he desperately needed that in his life. He needed her. It was still Christmas Eve morning. He reached for his phone and made arrangements to get the plane ready to fly to Dallas. He had to see Emma.

Christmas Eve at four in the afternoon Emma rushed back to her apartment. It was already getting dark outside with an overcast gray sky and a light snow predicted. Carrying an armload of packages, she hurried into her apartment building to be stopped by the doorman.

"Miss Hillman, you have a delivery."

Surprised, she waited while he disappeared into the office and returned with a red crystal vase that held several dozen red roses and stems of holly.

"That's for me?" she said, glancing at the packages filling her arms. "I'll come back to get it."

"I'll bring it up. I didn't want to leave it in the hall."

"Thank you." At her apartment she unlocked the door and stepped back to let him carry the bouquet inside and set it down.

"Merry Christmas, Miss Hillman. You have beautiful flowers."

"Thank you. Merry Christmas to you, Mr. Wilburton," she said, tipping him for carrying up her flowers.f

She dropped her packages and closed the door, hearing the lock click in place. The flowers had to be from Zach. She pulled out a card, looking at a familiar scrawling handwriting that she had seen so many times in the past few weeks.

"Merry Christmas, Emma. Zach." A pang rocked her. How she wished he were here! She missed him more each day and tried to avoid thinking about it if she could. With a glance at her watch, she realized she should get ready soon to join her family.

Hurrying to hang up her coat, she turned on her Christmas lights.

Lights sparkled on her tall green Douglas fir that held sparse ornaments, which she added to each Christmas. She had greenery and candles on her mantel, a wreath on her door and a dining room centerpiece of holly around the base of a large poinsettia that had been given to her by friends from her office.

This year she had added something new. She looked at the sprig of mistletoe she had hung above the doorway into the dining area. The mistletoe made her think of Zach and their mistletoe kisses. She wondered how he was enjoying his Italian villa. For all she knew, he might not be alone there.

Usually Christmas Eve filled her with anticipation and excitement, but this year she missed Zach and she could not keep from worrying about her baby and breaking the news to her family. In spite of her sister's reassurances, telling the family was going to be difficult, making her worry how they would take it. An even bigger concern was how Zach would accept the news.

She picked up all her packages to carry them to her bedroom and open them. She had been buying baby things because she was excited and wanted to get ready even if it was early. A bassinet stood by the window and she had a new rocking chair that had been delivered two days earlier. She began to open packages and finally had the new baby clothes laid out across her bed where she could look at them. They would all go into the wash, but she wanted to look at them first: the tiny onesies, tiny socks, little jumpers and bibs, rattles and a baby brush, plus small blankets.

She ran her fingers over the blankets. Even if Zach wanted to marry, which she knew he would not, she couldn't accept his lifestyle. He still wouldn't put family first. Travel and work would always take first place with him and fulfill the need for excitement in his life. It would never be family that would hold his interest. Sadness tinged her excitement over the baby. Sadness and worry about her baby's acceptance.

She showered to get ready to go to her parents' house for dinner and then a midnight service. Her new Christmas dress was a red crepe with a low V-neck and long sleeves. The skirt ended above her knees and she had matching high-heeled pumps. She caught her hair back on either side of her face and had clips with sprigs of holly attached. Last of all, she fastened the gold locket, stepping close to the mirror to look at it and rub the gold lightly with her finger as if she could conjure up Zach by doing so.

Startling her, her intercom buzzed. She answered to hear Mr. Wilburton.

"May I come back a moment? There's something else here."

"Sure, come up. I'll open the door," she answered, curious what he had. She gathered things to put into her purse until the bell rang. Wondering what he had forgotten, she hurried to the door to open it.

The first thing she saw was a huge stack of packages that hid the doorman.

"Come in," she said, wondering how Mr. Wilburton could have forgotten a mountain of gifts.

He turned slightly and she faced Zach. "Merry Christmas, Emma."

Stunned, she could only stare at him. "Zach? You're here? It's Christmas Eve. Where's Mr. Wilburton?"

Zach laughed. "These packages are getting heavy. Can I come in?"

Ten

"Come in," she said, her heart racing as she took presents off the top of his stack.

He rushed to her sofa to set them all down while she closed the door and trailed behind him. He was in a black topcoat over his suit. When he turned, she took one look in his eyes and she was in his arms. He had brought a rush of cold air in and his coat still was cold and smelled of the outside. As she slid her arms beneath his coat and jacket, he felt warm, holding her tightly against him while they kissed.

Her heart thudded with joy. Giddy to see him, laughter bubbled inside her. She was overwhelmed by surprise.

Desire raged, more than all else, and she pushed the topcoat away, hearing it fall to the floor. His suit jacket went with it. With shaking fingers, she unfastened the buttons to his snowy shirt. He held her away to look at her, taking in her red dress before he kissed her again.

Picking her up in his arms, Zach carried her to her bedroom while he kissed her. Emma clung to him, wrapped in his embrace and filled with longing. When he set her on her feet, she could feel his hands at the top of her zipper as he started to draw it down.

His hands grew still and he raised his head. "Is one of your sisters expecting?"

Startled, she looked up at him. "No, neither one." Zach looked beyond her at the bed and then his gaze went around the room and she realized why.

"Emma, that's a lot of baby clothes and a lot of baby things. More than you'd take to a shower."

His questioning gaze returned to her. Her heart drummed and her palms became damp. She hadn't expected Zach. All the most recent baby things were laid out. Her mouth went dry and she felt weak in the knees.

"I know only one way to tell you. I'm pregnant," she whispered.

"You're pregnant?" Sounding stunned, he stepped back to look at her. "You don't look it. You have all this ready for a baby. Are you sure? When are you due?"

"I've been to a doctor now. When I found out for certain, I couldn't wait to buy things. I know it's too early, Zach. I'm barely pregnant, but I'm excited. This isn't the way I was going to tell you, or this soon. I know you have your life and you're not the daddy type—"

"And you're not the single-mom type. I'm going to be a dad," he said and silence stretched between them. Suddenly his hands closed on her waist and he held her up while he gave a whoop.

"A dad! Emma, love," he said, setting her down and wrapping his arms around her to kiss her hard and long.

Shocked by his reaction, the last possible thing she had expected, she stood immobile for seconds until she caught her breath. Wrapping her arms around him, she held him tightly to kiss him back.

He stopped as abruptly as he started. "You're sure?"

"Absolutely. The doctor says yes. The pregnancy test was positive. My body is changing. Ask Rosie. And Mary Kate guessed."

"Rosie?" he said, looking stunned. "You knew then?"

"I suspected, but it was really early. Rosie did, too."

He laughed. "Emma, that's fabulous. We're going to be parents. My precious love, I came to ask you to marry me." He knelt on one knee and took her hand. "Emma Hillman, I love you and want you to be my wife. Will you marry me?"

"Zach, get up," she said, her smile fading because she hurt badly. He had just proposed, saying words she hadn't been able to avoid dreaming about, but there was only one answer. She looked up at him as he stood. "I love you and I'm thrilled and scared about the baby, but, Zach, we can't marry. Our lifestyles are poles apart. You wouldn't be happy. I wouldn't be happy with you gone all the time."

"Emma, we have to work this out," he said, framing her face with his hands. "I've been miserable without you. You've made me see a family can be happy and love each other. We'll work this out."

"I can't. You'll be gone and you do risky things. You won't be there to be a dad."

"Yes, I will," he said patiently. "And love isn't in one place or in a house. It's between two people. Your parents would have had the same love if your dad had traveled. You have to agree on that one."

"I guess they would have, but I don't want a dad who's gone all the time."

"I won't be. I can work more in the Dallas office and let others do the on-site requirements. For heaven's sake, I own the place. I don't have to go out and do hands-on work. I don't even have to work if I don't want to."

She didn't dare breathe as her whole being tingled and

hope flared. "You might not be happy with a desk job," she said, wondering if she dared accept his complete reversal of his lifestyle.

"I don't want to be away from you."

"You would do that?"

"Of course. Emma, you've made me open my heart and trust someone to return my love. Don't turn around and crush that now. I love you and I want to marry you. Besides that, it's been pure hell without you."

She trembled, wanting to believe him, scared to do so. "Rosie said you couldn't change."

"Well, there are some things Rosie doesn't know about me. She doesn't know I have fallen in love with the most wonderful woman in the world."

Unable to smile because of the moment for a life-changing decision, Emma stood looking into his eyes. They were both taking chances, but they loved each other and love was too precious to toss aside. As her decision came, she trembled. "Yes, I'll marry you," she answered, wrapping her arms around his neck to kiss him. Excitement and joy blossomed, enveloping her. Tears of happiness spilled down her cheeks.

"Don't cry. Not even happy tears," he said. "Darlin', this is too fabulous for even one tear. Marriage to you will be the most wonderful thing in my life. You're right, Emma. What counts in life is the people you love."

After a moment he raised his head. "How far along are you?"

"Just barely pregnant," she answered, smiling at him.

He looked beyond her at the bed covered in baby clothes. "Isn't this really premature?"

"It is, but I'm excited."

"And your family? They may not be happy with me, but when they hear we're getting married, they should be okay. Do you think?"

"They don't know. It's early, Zach. Mary Kate knows. She guessed and we're close so she asked me. No one else knows."

"Then don't tell them yet," he said. "Tonight let's announce we're getting married. Let's marry on Christmas." He smiled. "I don't want to wait any longer anyway."

"That's not possible, Zach. That's tomorrow."

"I know when Christmas is. Unless you have your heart set on a big wedding, we'll marry tomorrow with just your family. That's enough people to fill the church."

"What about your brothers and your half sister and her husband, whom you're close to?"

"Listen to me," he said. "We marry tomorrow. Then we're off on a honeymoon and I'll get you out of the state of Texas. First, the Italian villa and then Paris and back to New York, Niagra Falls and then home. How does that sound?"

"Impossible."

"No, it's not. We can get a church and just have the family and get married tomorrow afternoon. Then when we come back from a honeymoon we can have a big reception and invite everyone, including my family. We can announce the baby whenever you're ready."

Too thrilled to plan anything, she laughed. "It still sounds impossible. As a matter of fact, I have to be at my folks' home at six tonight. It's already after five."

"We have time to make some decisions. If you run late, you can call and tell them you're on your way."

"I go for the evening. We all eat there and then we go to midnight church service together. Will you go with me?"

He kissed her lightly on the forehead. "Of course, I'll go."

She smiled. "Why didn't you call me?" she asked, running her fingers over his shoulder.

"I should have, but I was going as fast as I could. I just decided to come this morning."

"You came from Italy?"

"No, I never did go to Italy," he said. "I missed you too much. Italy seemed empty and unappealing. My heart was here in Texas."

Her heart missed a beat as she gazed up at him. She combed her fingers through his thick hair. "I feel as if I haven't seen you for a long, long time."

"I know. That's the way I feel about you," he said. "I couldn't wait until New Year's Eve."

"I'm stunned," she said. "I thought you were in Italy. You said you were going."

"Italy lost its appeal and I kept putting it off until it seemed pointless to go. I've missed you," he said solemnly and another wave of happiness swamped her. She kissed him lightly on the lips.

"Zach, no one will marry us on such short notice, and not on Christmas."

"Sure they will," he replied. "Maybe you're not the optimist I thought you were. I think I can get our minister to do the ceremony. I'll call him unless you want to ask yours first."

"You get your minister. I can't imagine calling any minister on Christmas Eve and asking him to marry us on Christmas Day. That's wild, Zach," she said, dazed and unable to believe she was marrying him. "We don't have a license. We don't have what we need."

"I'll call my attorney and get him moving. He'll get it worked out. We can still marry in the church tomorrow."

"This is crazy. What'll I wear?"

"You'll look beautiful in whatever you wear and we can go from here to a dress shop and then to your parents' house. I know the perfect store and I'll see if they'll stay open until we get there."

She listened as he talked to his lawyer and her incredulity deepened. Everything seemed impossible. It was turning into a magical Christmas where the impossible became possible. Mrs. Zachary Delaney. Was she rushing headlong into disaster or into paradise? Right now, she viewed it as paradise. Zach had already made astounding changes in his life.

He called a store and talked briefly. "Grab what you need," he said to Emma. "They were just about to close, but she'll wait. You can find something you like there."

"What store?"

He told her the name of an exclusive shop that was far beyond her budget and she had never crossed the threshold even to look there.

"Zach, are you certain? We're really rushing into this and you just blithely said you'd change your whole way of living."

"I sure did. That's how much I love you. Wait a minute." He rummaged through the mound of presents he had brought with him and returned swiftly to hand her a gift in a small box wrapped in green foil paper with a red ribbon and sprigs of artificial mistletoe in the bow.

"It's too pretty to open."

"Open it. What's inside may be prettier."

She opened it with shaking fingers and he caught her hand. "You're shaking."

She looked up. "I'm thrilled and happy and so in love. And my whole life is changing before my eyes. I'm scared."

He hugged her. "I love you, Emma," he said quietly and firmly in his deep voice. "Truly love you with all my heart and want to make you happy. You think I want to be off blowing up some building when I can be home in bed with you every night?"

She laughed while tears stung her eyes. He tilted her face up. "Don't cry, love. I love you and I don't want to ever hurt you."

"Tears of joy, Zach," she whispered, wiping her eyes. She opened the box and a dazzling diamond glittered in the light. "Zach, it's magnificent," she gasped.

He removed the ring and placed it on her finger. "Emma, will you marry me?" he asked again.

"Yes, Zach," she said and kissed him.

In seconds he released her. "We better run."

"Let me think. You've got me so rattled. I'm supposed to be taking something to my parents. It's a chocolate cheesecake from the fridge. Let me get it."

She hurried to the kitchen and returned to the living room where she stopped to look at her sofa. "Zach, what are all these presents?"

"They're your Christmas presents from me. I had the ones for your family sent out to your parents' house."

"How'd you know you'd even be invited?"

He grinned. "C'mon. Someone's holding open a store for us."

She shook her head as she pulled on her coat. He carried the chocolate cheesecake that was in a plastic container.

He had a limo waiting and she climbed into the back. The limo gave her pause, a sobering moment, because it brought back how much Zach was worth. "Zach, you are part of the Delaney fortune that has been well publicized. I don't see a bodyguard."

"I have one at times. He's not with us now because our driver can cover if needed, but Will's the one in the limelight. I'm not in papers and haven't been in the country lately. Ryan could pass for any cowboy in west Texas. He's not in papers a lot either. Besides that, Ryan's a tough cowboy and he looks like the type to be packing. If I were going after a Delaney, I'd put Ryan at the bottom of the list. Ryan and I are both low-key and I don't feel threatened."

"I'm thinking about your baby."

"Don't worry about it. I'll have all the security you and I both feel we need. A baby is different. We'll have plenty of security."

She realized her life was changing drastically as she looked at her fiancé whom she loved with all her being. She pulled out her cell phone. "I want to call and let Mom and Dad know you're coming with me. Then it won't be a surprise when you walk in."

"Good idea. My presents should have arrived."

In minutes she put away her phone. "They'll be glad to see you. And they did get your presents. How in the world did you know what to buy? And how many to buy for?"

"Someone told me how many were eating Thanksgiving dinner. How many adults and how many kids. They're sort of generic presents. Electronic games for the kids, baskets of fruit for the adults."

She laughed. "Zach, our house will be buried under baskets of fruit."

He grinned and hugged her. Emma held out her hand to look at her ring. "This is the most gorgeous, giant ring I have ever seen."

"I'm glad you like it." He placed his arm around her. "Emma, I read some of the family letters. I got a touching one that you'll have to read. I saw what you were talking about. Somehow with that one letter, I actually did feel a tie to my great-great-grandfather."

"I'm glad, Zach," she said with another increase in her happiness. "I was going to ask for any of the letters you decided to shred because I'll be the mother of a Delaney. And this little Delaney is going to grow up with a love and appreciation of family."

"The mother of a Delaney, my baby's mother," he said. "That sounds wonderful to me. You've given me the best possible Christmas gift I've ever received," he whispered and pulled her close to kiss her. Pausing, he framed her face with his hands. "Emma, you've made up for all those miserable Christmases I had as kid. Will told me once to hang on, that our lives would get better."

"Zach, that makes me hurt for all three of you. But that's all in the past. You'll have so much family stirring around you on holidays, you may miss your solitude."

"No, I won't. Not as long as I have you," he said and kissed her again.

When the limo parked, Zach climbed out to help Emma. "You get whatever you want in here. I'm buying it for you, so don't even ask a price."

The second dress they brought out, a white raw silk with thin straps and a short jacket, was the one. The skirt was slim and came to mid-calf. She liked it immediately and in minutes she said that was the one she wanted. She didn't want Zach to see it until their wedding, so when she came out of the dressing room once again in her Christmas dress, his eyebrows arched.

"What's this?"

"I've picked the dress I want and you're not to see it until tomorrow."

"You've set a record for the fastest woman shopper I've ever seen. I'm falling in love all over again."

She laughed, but she wondered how many women he had taken shopping. In minutes they parked at her parents' house.

"This has to be the most decorated block in all of the state of Texas," Zach said, stepping into bright lights from her parents' decorations.

"Dad started this and then our neighbors began to get into the spirit."

"Thank heaven I'll be able to afford to have someone do ours for us," he said, eyeing her roof. As they walked to the front door, she felt butterflies in her stomach. "Zach, I feel jittery about tonight and having a wedding so fast tomorrow."

"Your family will accept what you want to do," he said.

"Would you rather take your time, marry later and have a big wedding?"

She thought a moment. "No, this is exciting and I think marrying tomorrow is a great idea. We're rushing into this—something I never thought I'd do."

"We're getting married tomorrow—something I never thought *I'd* do," he said with a broad smile and she laughed.

"Let's break the news. Get ready for a hullabaloo," she warned and opened the front door.

"You're right there."

As they walked inside, her dad came forward to greet them. Emma grasped her father's arm. "Dad, get Mom to come here. It's important."

With a glance at Zach, Brody turned to send a granddaughter on the errand and in seconds Emma's mother walked up to greet them and welcome Zach. Family members trailed after her, gathering around them.

"Mom, Dad, before someone notices and asks—Zach has asked me to marry him and I've accepted," she said, holding out her hand to show her engagement ring.

Instantly her mother hugged her while her dad shook hands with Zach and in seconds the whole family huddled around while Emma showed them her engagement ring.

From that moment on she felt as if she were in a dream. She spent an hour on phone calls, making arrangements that she couldn't believe were happening so quickly. She went through dinner in a daze and felt that way afterwards. Constantly, she was aware of Zach, even if he stood across the room. When they drove to church all the kids piled into the limo with them.

"Your life will change drastically," Emma reminded him.

"It already has," he remarked, eyeing the kids surrounding him.

Through the midnight Christmas service Zach sat close beside her. Finally they told everyone good-night and left.

"Emma, you've never even seen my home. Not any of them. Let's go back to my house tonight and I'll take you home as early in the morning as you want."

"All right. Is this where I'm going to live?"

"That's up to you. If you want a new place, I don't care. I got the Dallas place because it's comfortable and a good investment. If you want something else, fine."

"I hope you're always this agreeable."

He smiled. "I'll try. I want to call Ryan and Will. I should call Garrett, too. I want you to meet Ryan and Garrett and Sophia when we get back. I don't expect any of them to come home tomorrow. When we get back from our honeymoon, we can repeat our vows in a big church wedding if you want."

She shook her head. "I'm happy. Let's just have the reception and invite everyone. That'll be a party for all."

His limo entered an exclusive gated suburban area with a gatekeeper. As they wound through the neighborhood, through pines and oaks, she glimpsed twinkling lights indicating homes. Finally they went through another tall iron gate with a gatekeeper who waved.

"I guess I didn't need to worry so much about security."

"I have security. The family ranch is more open, but we had security around the perimeter of the yard and motion lights outside, with someone watching the grounds at night. You just didn't notice."

"You didn't tell me that," she said.

He shrugged. "I didn't expect you to leave in the dead of night without me knowing about it."

In minutes she could see lights through trees on a mansion and when it came into full view, her breath caught. "This is home?" she asked. "It's a resort hotel."

"No, it's not and we can move if you want. You'll see. It's comfortable inside."

"I can imagine," she said, unable to grasp that after tomorrow this would be her home. One of her homes.

"I feel like Cinderella," she whispered.

"And I feel like the luckiest man on earth," he said. "I called ahead and told them we were coming."

"Zach, I'm just now seeing your Dallas home. This reinforces that we barely know each other."

"I know what I want," he replied solemnly. "It's you, Emma, with all my heart. This is a house, maybe big and fancy, but it's just a house I have because of those ancestors you've been reading about and feeling so close to. You know my history, my family, my secrets, my work, me. We know each other. I know your family, your very open book growing up in a happy, loving family. Maybe you're right and you're the wealthier of the two of us," he said with a smile. "We know each other well enough. Our love will cover the rest and discovery sounds wonderful."

She hugged and kissed him briefly and then turned to look at the house. "I'm overwhelmed."

"You'll get used to the place. Nigel will work here when we return from our honeymoon. Rosie sort of goes from family to family."

They stepped out of the limo at the side of the mansion. At the door he unlocked it, picked her up and carried her inside. Setting her on her feet, he turned off the alarm.

"Now the quick tour. When we return from our honeymoon, you can have the full tour of the place."

Dazzled, she felt in a dream once again. They walked through an enormous kitchen with rich, dark wood hiding appliances, granite countertops, a smooth stone floor that held small area rugs. The adjoining informal eating area was as large as the kitchen.

Zach took her hand. "This way. You can look as we go and I'll show you around better later."

They climbed winding stairs and walked down a wide hall that held a strip of thick beige carpet down the center. Zach's bedroom was an enormous suite and the moment she stepped inside, she barely glimpsed polished oak floors, elegant fruitwood furniture and a wide-screen built into a wall.

"Come here. I called this afternoon and told my staff to put this up. Next year I'm sure we'll be as decorated as Rockefeller Center." He led her to a doorway between the sitting room and his bedroom with a massive four-poster king bed. Mistletoe hung in the doorway overhead and Zach stopped beneath it.

"I love you and I can't wait to marry you. In my heart we're already husband and wife," he said.

Her heart thudded with happiness as she hugged him while she kissed him beneath the mistletoe.

Epilogue

"Zach, I still feel like this isn't really happening to me," she said, thinking that was the way she had felt most of the time when they had been in Europe on their honeymoon. She looked at herself in the mirror, her gaze going beyond her image to Zach's. He looked incredibly handsome in his navy suit.

"My love is real, Emma," he said, brushing a kiss and his warm breath on her nape.

"All those wonderful cities and the charming small towns in France, Switzerland, Germany and Italy. They were beautiful and the people were welcoming. The places and buildings were breathtaking, so beautiful. Ah, Zach, I saw them all because of you. I will treasure the memories we have of this trip forever. It was wonderful to go and now it's grand to be home."

"The next long trip will be in this country. I want to show you special places in the U.S."

She smiled. "I'm nervous about meeting Ryan tonight."

Zach laughed. "Of all people on this earth, don't be nervous over Ryan. He's as down to earth as any man can get. He would have flown in to meet you earlier this week when we returned, but he had a bull-riding show in Wyoming or Montana. I don't remember where. Don't be nervous about any of them. Sophia is almost as new to the family as you are. I think you two will become good friends."

"Do you still want to tell my family the news about the baby when we go for Sunday dinner tomorrow?" she asked.

"Yes, unless you want to tell them tonight. We'll tell them and my family and anyone else you want to let know."

"Rosie, even though she guessed, and Nigel."

"Sure. All my staff will be told. I want everyone watching out for you."

She laughed. "Don't make it sound as if I'm an invalid. Let's tell them tomorrow."

"I love you, sweet wife," he whispered and kissed her.

She kissed him passionately, in seconds forgetting the evening until he reached for the zipper of her dress.

"Zach, we have a wedding reception to attend," she said, wriggling away from him and smiling.

"So we do, but I'd rather make love."

"Later," she said.

"Can't wait," he replied. "I'm ready and I'll wait downstairs. You look absolutely gorgeous."

"So do you, Zach," she said, her heart beating with happiness.

An hour later she stood in a country club ballroom talking to Sophia and Ava when she saw Zach and his brother approach. Ryan was tall, handsome, dressed in a black suit and wearing black Western boots.

"Finally you'll meet my brother Ryan. Ryan, meet Emma, my bride."

Ryan hugged her and kissed her cheek. "Welcome to the Delaney family," he said.

"Thank you," she answered. "All of you have made me feel welcome."

Zach clasped his brother on the shoulder. "Ladies, congratulate a champion bull rider. He just won again."

Ryan grinned as he received congratulations and Emma marveled again that the Delaneys resembled each other except for Zach. She couldn't see any similarities in his looks and theirs.

She saw Will and Garrett approaching and their circle enlarged. Will draped his arm around Ava's shoulders. "Caroline is playing with your nieces and nephews and your sister Mary Kate is with them," he said. "I told her to call my cell if I need to come get her."

"Caroline will be fine and Mary Kate loves being with the kids."

The band commenced another song and Ryan turned to Emma. "May I have this dance? If I want to get to know you, we have to get away from this crowd."

She laughed and went with him the short distance to join the dancers.

"You've worked a miracle with my brother," Ryan said. "Will and I are delighted. Sophia hasn't been in this family long enough to know how much he'd changed."

"I love Zach and I want him to be happy."

"He is. You're good for him. Will and I wouldn't have thought it was possible to get him to settle down even a little. You have a great family. I've met most of them. I told all of them to bring their kids out to my ranch and let them ride. We have gentle horses. I think Connor is going to take me up first and bring his boys."

"I'm sure they'll love it. That's nice."

He spun her around and she glanced at Zach, already wanting the reception to be over and to be alone with him again.

When the dance ended, the group had broken up and Zach waited. "You've spent enough time with her, so goodbye, Ryan," Zach said, taking her hand.

"Thanks for the dance. I don't know how he talked you into marrying him," he teased. "Try to put up with him."

She laughed. "I think I can put up with him. It was nice to meet you, Ryan."

Zach led her to the dance floor to take her into his arms. "I'm ready for this to be over now."

"So am I," she said, gazing into his blue eyes that were as fascinating as the first day she met him. "I love you so," she whispered.

He pulled her close to wrap his arms around her and she danced slowly with him while her happiness bubbled. Her wonderful husband and their baby on the way—joy overflowed and she squeezed him. "Zach, this is paradise," she whispered, and he smiled at her, his eyes filled with warmth and love.

* * * * *

REQUEST YOUR FREE BOOKS!
2 FREE NOVELS PLUS 2 FREE GIFTS!

Harlequin® *Desire*

ALWAYS POWERFUL, PASSIONATE AND PROVOCATIVE

YES! Please send me 2 FREE Harlequin Desire® novels and my 2 FREE gifts (gifts are worth about $10). After receiving them, if I don't wish to receive any more books, I can return the shipping statement marked "cancel." If I don't cancel, I will receive 6 brand-new novels every month and be billed just $4.30 per book in the U.S. or $4.99 per book in Canada. That's a saving of at least 14% off the cover price! It's quite a bargain! Shipping and handling is just 50¢ per book in the U.S. and 75¢ per book in Canada.* I understand that accepting the 2 free books and gifts places me under no obligation to buy anything. I can always return a shipment and cancel at any time. Even if I never buy another book, the two free books and gifts are mine to keep forever.

225/326 HDN FEF3

Name	(PLEASE PRINT)
Address	Apt. #
City	State/Prov.	Zip/Postal Code

Signature (if under 18, a parent or guardian must sign)

Mail to the **Reader Service:**
IN U.S.A.: P.O. Box 1867, Buffalo, NY 14240-1867
IN CANADA: P.O. Box 609, Fort Erie, Ontario L2A 5X3

Not valid for current subscribers to Harlequin Desire books.

Want to try two free books from another line?
Call 1-800-873-8635 or visit www.ReaderService.com.

* Terms and prices subject to change without notice. Prices do not include applicable taxes. Sales tax applicable in N.Y. Canadian residents will be charged applicable taxes. Offer not valid in Quebec. This offer is limited to one order per household. All orders subject to credit approval. Credit or debit balances in a customer's account(s) may be offset by any other outstanding balance owed by or to the customer. Please allow 4 to 6 weeks for delivery. Offer available while quantities last.

Your Privacy—The Reader Service is committed to protecting your privacy. Our Privacy Policy is available online at www.ReaderService.com or upon request from the Reader Service.

We make a portion of our mailing list available to reputable third parties that offer products we believe may interest you. If you prefer that we not exchange your name with third parties, or if you wish to clarify or modify your communication preferences, please visit us at www.ReaderService.com/consumerschoice or write to us at Reader Service Preference Service, P.O. Box 9062, Buffalo, NY 14269. Include your complete name and address.

Harlequin® Desire is proud to present

ONE WINTER'S NIGHT

by New York Times *bestselling author*

Brenda Jackson

Alpha Blake tightened her coat around her. Not only would she be late for her appointment with Riley Westmoreland, but because of her flat tire they would have to change the location of the meeting and Mr. Westmoreland would be the one driving her there. This was totally embarrassing, when she had been trying to make a good impression.

She turned up the heat in her car. Even with a steady stream of hot air coming in through the car vents, she still felt cold, too cold, and wondered if she would ever get used to the Denver weather. Of course, it was too late to think about that now. It was her first winter here, and she didn't have any choice but to grin and bear it. When she'd moved, she'd felt that getting as far away from Daytona Beach as she could was essential to her peace of mind. But who in her right mind would prefer blistering-cold Denver to sunny Daytona Beach? Only a person wanting to start a new life and put a painful past behind her.

Her attention was snagged by an SUV that pulled off the road and parked in front of her. The door swung open and long denim-clad, boot-wearing legs appeared before a man stepped out of the truck. She met his gaze through the windshield and forgot to breathe. Walking toward her car was a man who was so dangerously masculine, so heart-stoppingly virile, that her brain went momentarily numb.

He was tall, and the Stetson on his head made him appear taller. But his height was secondary to the sharp

HDEXP1212

handsomeness of his features.

Her gaze slid all over him as he moved his long limbs toward her vehicle in a walk that was so agile and self-assured, she envied the confidence he exuded with every step. Her breasts suddenly peaked, and she could actually feel blood rushing through her veins.

She didn't have to guess who this man was.

He was Riley Westmoreland.

Find out if Riley and Alpha mix business with pleasure in

ONE WINTER'S NIGHT

by Brenda Jackson

Available December 2012

Only from Harlequin® Desire

SPECIAL EDITION

Life, Love and Family

NEW YORK TIMES BESTSELLING AUTHOR

DIANA PALMER

brings you a brand-new Western romance
featuring characters that readers have come to
love—the Brannt family from Harlequin HQN's
bestselling book *WYOMING TOUGH*.

Cort Brannt, Texas rancher through and through,
is about to unexpectedly get lassoed by love!

THE RANCHER

Available November 13 wherever books are sold!

Also available as a 2-in-1
THE RANCHER & HEART OF STONE